The Enchanter's Mirror
and Other Stories

The Enchanter's Mirror
and Other Stories

by
Marie-Antoinette Fagnan

Translated, annotated and introduced by
Brian Stableford

A Black Coat Press Book

Visit our website at www.blackcoatpress.com

ISBN 978-1-61227-820-9. First Printing. January 2019. Published by Black Coat Press, an imprint of Hollywood Comics.com, LLC, P.O. Box 17270, Encino, CA 91416.

TABLE OF CONTENTS

Introduction

Kanor, conte traduit du sauvage par Madame ** was first published in 1750, allegedly in Amsterdam, but almost certainly in Paris. "Minet-bleu et Louvette" was originally published in the *Mercure de France* in September 1750 with the signature "Madame de Fagnan," accompanied by an editorial note identifying that person as the author of *Kanor*. *Le Miroir des princesses orientales*, here translated as "The Enchanter's Mirror," was first published in 1755, without any indication of a publisher or a place of publication, but with the signature "Madame Fagnan."

The catalogue of the Bibliothèque Nationale also credits to Madame Fagnan *Histoire et aventures de Mylord Pet, conte allégorique, par Madame F***, was published as a booklet in 1755, allegedly in The Hague by "Gosse Junior" (a joke) but almost certainly in Paris; the text is now reproduced on *gallica*. The actual title has "Milord" rather than "Mylord," so the catalogue entry is mistaken. Although it is not strictly relevant to the present collection I have included it as an appendix so that readers can make up their own minds whether it is conceivable that it is the work of the author of *Le Miroir des princesses orientales*, and can judge, in consequence, the reliability of the Bibliothèque Nationale's bibliographical attributions.

Appearances suggest strongly that *Histoire et aventures de Milord Pet*, unlike *Le Miroir des princesses orientales*, is by a male author—it seems highly unlikely that any female author in the 1750s would ever have

7

dreamed of publishing such a story—and that the F in the signature is far more likely to stand for "Fesse" [buttock], that being the signature on the satirically comical dedication, than the name of a real person, and that the appellation Madame results purely from the circumstance that Fesse is a feminine noun. The point is of some significance, because the attribution of the other three stories does not seem entirely convincing to me either, even though numerous reference books, like the Bibliothèque Nationale catalogue, have reproduced it mechanically from its single original source.

In particular, it is worth pointing out that the dedication to the Marquise de Pompadour in *Le Miroir des princesses orientales* is curious, in a work that appears to have been published without the royal privilege necessary for licit publication, and with a full signature, given that such works were almost always discreetly anonymous; it is not entirely obvious whether the dedication ought to be interpreted sincerely or sarcastically, but probability inclines toward the latter hypothesis.

In 1755 the Marquise de Pompadour (1721-1764) was no longer Louis XV's "official chief mistress," as she had been between 1745 and 1751, but she still had abundant influence at court. She had a reputation as a patroness of the arts and of the *philosophes*, the acquaintance of many of whom she had made in the early days of her marriage to Charles Le Normant d'Étiolles, contracted in 1740, when she attended several of the most celebrated salons in Paris and briefly hosted her own, attended by Montesquieu and Voltaire among others. She might well have met "Madame Fagnan" at that time, and certainly met other writers engaged in the "contraband renaissance" of *contes de fées*, including the Comte de Caylus and Charles Duclos. However, a sincerely fulsome dedication of an illicit work to the Marquise would have been indiscreet, to say the least, especially if an authentic signature were attached to it—and the great rarity of such signatures surely casts doubt on its authenticity. The signature and note attached to the *Mercure de France* publication of "Minet-bleu et Louvette" does appear to establish that the three stories attributed to "Madame Fagnan" are by the same person, but the fact that she could not make up her mind whether the name had a *particule* or not does not add confidence to the supposition that it was her real name.

All subsequent comments regarding "Madame Fagnan" appear to be based on the account of her work included by Joseph de La Porte in his *Histoires des femmes qui se sont rendues célébres dans la littérature* (1769). La Porte reports that he had been told that her husband worked in "some bureau," but that that was all he had been able to learn about a woman who "appeared to prefer a peaceful obscurity to the literary celebrity that she might have flattered herself with obtaining." There are, in fact, very few references to any Madame Fagnan in other eighteenth century works not derived from La Porte's annotation, but one significant exception is a passage in the memoirs of the Venetian playwright Carlo Goldoni (1707-1793), who was the director of the Théâtre Italien in Paris from 1761 onwards, and wrote most of his subsequent works in French, and with whom La Porte was certainly acquainted. Although the memoirs were not published until 1787, it is not impossible that Goldoni mentioned verbally to La Porte that he had met a Madame Fagnan, who was the widow of a principal secretary of the royal treasury, and that La Porte jumped to the conclusion that she was the author of the three stories—a claim that Goldoni does not make in his memoirs. Goldoni does not mention his Madame Fagnan's forenames, either, but it is not improbable that he supplied them, either to La Porte or to Charles-Joseph Mayer, for his annotation of the author in volume 37 of his *Cabinet des fées* (1786), for want of any other plausible source of that item of information.

Whether or not La Porte was correct in attributing the three works to the actual Madame Fagnan, however, they certainly comprise a very interesting addition to the contraband renaissance of *contes de fées*, and provide strong evidence of that fact that the renaissance in question had already reached its decadence by the early 1750s. The tone of such tales had been apologetic from the beginning of the renaissance in the late 1730s, well aware of the fact that there was a certain awkwardness in accommodating such tales to the *zeitgeist* of a burgeoning Age of Enlightenment. In fact, however, as Madame Fagnan demonstrated as well as anyone, the literary fantastic could be a useful instrument in the advancement of Enlightenment, because rather than in spite of its manifest absurdity—by no means as bad a thing in literature as in logic.

The sardonic narrative voice of *Kanor* goes to some lengths to point out the absurdity of the conventions of the *conte de fees*, and to emphasize that the age of the fays, if ever there was one, must have reached its twilight long before history became possible. Nevertheless, the story makes significant and constructive use of the fay Fierotine and the ingenuity of her enchantments in contriving a plot that is amusing, highly unusual and, in spite of its moderate length—nicely labyrinthine.

Contemporary readers doubtless noticed—some of them commented on the fact in print—that the satirical opening of the story appears to have been inspired by

Jonathan Swift's account of the travels of Lemuel Gulliver, and more than one subsequent critic opined that it seemed a shame that the satirical element of the story, summarized in the determination of the shrunken king Alzopha to diminish all his subjects to a height that would make it feasible for him to continue to rule them, was abandoned in favor of the tale's eccentric celebration of the power of amour, something that neither Gulliver nor Swift would ever have endorsed. However, an intense focus on the supposed properties and power of "*amour parfait*" had been a foundation-stone of *contes de fées* since their invention, and might well have been an element of their preparatory manifesto; in joining the contraband renaissance, Madame Fagnan was evidently entering the lists scrupulously, with the same esthetic equipage as her predecessors.

"Minette-bleu et Louvette" confirms that supposition, as well as making very evident the ideological pressure that was exerted on the writers of the contraband renaissance by the contemporaneity of the *philosophes*. Some of the writers involved in that renaissance were *philosophes* themselves, and all of the others appear to have personally acquainted with *philosophes* that they met on the salon circuit; even those who did not actually encounter Voltaire and Montesquieu, and surely did not initially read their tales in their presence, would undoubtedly have had them in mind as hypothetical addressees. Madame Fagnan clearly took that consciousness to heart, and "Minette-bleu et Louvette" is a manifest literary thought-experiment, in which the conventional perversities of fay magic are employed as a means to establish an awkward situation that requires authorial ingenuity as well as the power of amour to reach its desired conclusion.

The kind of fays invented and developed by the coterie of female writers surrounding Madame d'Aulnoy and the Comtesse de Murat still had an evident utility in the construction of such plots in 1755, but they no longer had the near-monopoly that they had briefly enjoyed as agents of enchantment in the 1690s. Voltaire only mentioned fays in passing, finding the imaginative apparatus of pseudo-Oriental fantasy more useful for his own purposes, and borrowing eclectically from other mythologies, including the Christian mythos, when such elements seemed more apt. The other *philosophes* who made prolific use of literary fantasy in modeling their ideas—most notably Louis-Sébastien Mercier—shunned fays even more rigorously. Most of the writers of the contraband renaissance of *contes de fées*, including such luminaries as Mademoiselle de Lubert and the Comte de Caylus, had abandoned them by 1755, and Madame Fagnan was no exception to the rule, although her longest and most interesting fantasy retains a male enchanter as its agent and only makes tokenistic gestures in the direction of Oriental fantasy, hardly constituting the thinnest of masks. However, the brief rant that begins part two of that story is a significant and telling signpost in the steep decline of the fays.

The real subject-matter of *Le Miroir des princesses orientales*, of course, is not the magic mirror of the title, which merely provides the crucial lever that moves the plot at key moments. The heart of the enterprise, as with the later part of *Kanor* and the entire tradition of *contes de fées* that lay behind the two novellas, is the operation within the human heart of amour—here far more weakly personalized than in *Kanor*, almost completely reduced to something more like an instinct than a god, although no less tyrannical for that. Madame Fagnan was by no means the first writer to introduce a strong dose of anxious skepticism into her account of the likely effects of amour on human life and ambition—that worm had been imported to the genre's bud by Catherine Bernard and Mademoiselle de La Force, and had never seemed likely to die of starvation—but *Le Miroir des princesses orientales* is certainly one of the most striking and one of the most heartfelt displays of that skepticism, emphasizing in no uncertain terms the enormous difficulty of attaining the "happy ending" written into the manifesto of the genre and the consequent unlikelihood of its attainment.

The motto that concludes *Kanor*, which boldly claims that Amour can work miracles, is fundamental to the entire genre, but "Minette-bleu et Louvette" focuses more intently on the complication of the miracle-working required, and the tripartite plot and eventual conclusion of *Le Miroir des princesses orientales* add the uncomfortable rider that, in order to achieve the desired conclusion of a *conte de fées*, nothing less than a miracle is likely do the job.

Madame Fagnan's work as a whole asserts and emphasizes that hypothetical fays are not, and never could be, up to the task of providing such miracles routinely, because the inevitably corrupting effects of such power would always be likely to lead them to indifference to human suffering, if not to the malevolence of causing it. That, rather than any vulgar scientific skepticism relating to the workability of magic, is the Enlightenment that hammered the nails into the coffin of the genre, and although the final nail had yet to be added, that coffin was already firmly sealed by 1755, and Madame Fagnan, whoever she might have been, was one of the most significant and most accurate hammer-wielding undertakers.

As for the history and adventures of Milord Pet, what is there to say about a story that speaks so eloquently and scatologically for itself? The amorous vagaries of the human heart do not enter into the narrative at all, its symbolic aim being far lower, and it is probably safe to say that if "Madame Fagnan" had been able to imagine for an instant that she would ever be suspected—and by the Bibliothèque Nationale!—of having written it, she would have suffered a nasty attack of what was known in those days as "the vapors."

The translations of *Kanor* and *Le Miroir des princesses orientales* were made from the versions of the text available on Google Books. The translation of "Minet-bleu et Louvette" was made from the version reprinted in Charles-Joseph Mayer's *Cabinet des fées* and reproduced on the Bibliothèque Nationale's *gallica* website. The translation of *Histoire et aventures de Milord Pet* was also made from the copy reproduced on *gallica*.

Brian Stableford.

KANOR: A TALE TRANSLATED FROM THE SAVAGE

Foreword

An ancient and entire savage manuscript is a very rare item, because it is neither writing, nor design, nor punctures, nor knots that forms the characters, which consist uniquely of certain creases and grimaces formed on the large leaves of trees, on small pieces of bark, on sheets of some metals and fish bones, or a few pieces of fabric cut, frayed, folded and refolded in every fashion, with the consequence that whatever intelligence one has of the language, if one loses a grimace or misses a crease, one loses the thread of a work, the finesse of a thought, and the meaning of an author. If, therefore, you find anything displeasing, if anything that lacks sense and coherence, in this work, it is neither the fault of the original nor mine; it is a consequence of some missing crease, some shred of bark or some lost fragment of cloth.

You can easily imagine that the appearance of one of these savage manuscripts is a prodigious mass of rags; the more ancient it is, and, for that reason, the more precious, the less one is tempted to take possession of it. It is thus that unrefined gold or diamonds appear to be vile matter in the eyes of those who do not know how to recognize them.

Similarly, you will understand what I am trying to convey: that it is fortunate to encounter an item so rare, and so difficult to conserve. In order to obtain the advantage of that good fortune, it requires a great deal of care, skill and toil in gathering and organizing so many separate pieces; all of that enabled me to succeed, and turn it to my profit, with the result that it forms the foundation of an almost full preface.

One essential thing remains for me to say; I almost forgot it, in which I would have resembled the compilers of many prefaces. It is that, in a savage foreword in which the author praises himself, as is only just, he declares that there is no hidden meaning or allegory in his work. He considers the perpetual seekers of malign allusions to be enemies of the veritable taste that ought to reign over these sorts of works; he sustains and proves, in a savant fashion that is not appropriate to me, that one can please by means of interest, the charm of images, the finesse of sentiment, the variety and the verity of colors, and the finesse of style, independently of all allegory. Will he please in the same way in our language? I don't know; but the purity of his intentions has pleased me and has determined me to prefer it to a number of contemporary savages who have written in the same taste.

Now that all is said, I am taking my bits of bark in hand, arranging my flowers, my fruits, my leaves and my rags, and it is no longer me who is speaking; I am translating.

I

Once—which is to say, a long time ago, shortly after the Deluge, so to speak—two savage peoples lived on the banks of the famous Amazon River. They were almost not savage, because the whole world was; fashion softens everything; although savage by comparison with us and the fashions of today, they were nevertheless domesticated, polite, and even gallant for that time. Do we not still have, amid our politeness, a certain savage gallantry? Why should they not have had a gallant ferocity? The distance of places and times makes little difference; people resemble one another, and are much more similar in the foundation of their mores than they think.

Those people did not have the brilliant exterior that promises so much and often renders very little, and yet is decisive; they were simple and almost naked; friends of truth and nature, they had a heart, and they followed its movements; sentiment took the place of intellect for them, and did not lead them astray. Happier in their simplicity and their ignorance than we are by virtue of our knowledge and our finesse, they spent their lives enjoying things, instead of wasting them desiring things.

The savages in question lived near the mouth of the river. They each had a king, that king had a court, and in spite of the happy simplicity of the peoples, the two courts had a small number of courtiers, a certain quantity of flatterers, a few liars, one or two physicians, a few spies, several hypocrites, pearls, diamonds, popinjays, prudes and coquettes, ugly by day and beautiful by night—all of it, of course, in the savage manner and taste.

Kanor was the king of one of those peoples, Alzopha was the sovereign of the other; although they were neighbors, they were friends, which was already fine and rare—all the more reason why it would be a fine rarity if it were ever encountered today. Their kingdoms were only separated by the river that irrigates and divides that vast region and flows into the sea.

Their subjects, following the example of their sovereigns, lived in good intelligence; the interest that divides and burns like fire did not cause quarrels between them; detachments of the two nations often went hunting and fishing together; the produce was shared fairly and without trickery. They went on expeditions by sea, and when they did not encounter enemy boats to pillage they avenged themselves on the sea-cows with which the beaches were covered.

The Kanoris were prompt and frank, the Alzophages more refined, more temperate and more prudent, very similar to our Normans and Picards. Although the atmospheric temperature was mild, the Alzophages wore clothes and the Kanoris went semi-naked. That is not astonishing; among us we have people of both sexes who are very well-covered, others who wear very little, and others who wear nothing at all; it is not cold or warmth that determines that. Each of those peoples found grace and advantages in their attire.

One day, when the two kings had given a fête, half-savage and half-gallant, at which their courts had amused themselves greatly, without really knowing why, in the manner that courts amused themselves those days, in order to conclude such a fine day, Kanor proposed an excursion at sea. There was a kind of challenge between the two boats that the sovereigns and the ladies of the court were manning, as to which would make a better catch of fish. Alzopha was aboard a small, light boat with an excellent soft yellow Martin varnish;[1] Kanor was commanding a lilac brigantine with an aventurine bottom, nicely indented with toothed edges and decorated with a sculpture in bas-relief, which formed a tasteful flower-stand.

The ladies were arranged in a semicircle at one of the ends of each boat, sitting on rich triangular cushions, in accordance with local custom. Those who had voices were singing Kanori songs, very similar to our Italian arias, for which they had a strong liking. The lords, who were connoisseurs of music, or thought they were, accompanied them with those little well-turned sniggers that are worth more, at certain moments, than the best-chosen things said with an ill grace. The ladies who were not singing were making knots. The moon was shining, the air was cool and serene; the night had the tender and piquant atmosphere that it only has when it is beautiful and the company enjoying it is select.

Suddenly, the sailors charged with extending the nets cried that they were no longer able to retain them, so heavily laden were they. The same thing happened almost simultaneously on both boats. Everyone hastened to help them, in order to draw then nets in promptly. Both nets were full of oysters, and nothing else. The only difference was that the oysters caught by the small yellow boat were all very small, while those on the lilac brigantine, on the contrary, were very large—which seemed singular. They were also very surprised that

---

[1] "Martin varnish," named for its French popularizer, who imported the idea from the Far East in the early eighteenth century, involved the addition of powdered gold or bronze to the varnish in order to give it a metallic sheen.

those shellfish were found assembled so far from the shore. One of the extraordinary mollusks was opened on each vessel; the little one contained a very small oyster and a very large pearl; the big one contained a very large oyster but a very small pearl. The difference in the catches put those who were less well-treated in a bad mood; the boats separated coldly and each returned to its own terrain.

Alzopha thought that he ought not to take his eyes off the little oysters because of the big pearls; he nominated a few of his favorites and lords in who he had the most confidence to help him open them; those that were to be opened for supper were set aside, and the rest were put in a safe place. As people of quality in every land are not ignorant of anything, all the lords of the court understood cooking perfectly, without having learned it. They therefore amused themselves making a hundred little whimsical concoctions and putting the open oysters into twenty Alzophage sauces.

In the meantime, the queen, whose name was Brazile and who was reputed to be a princess of superior merit, was playing with some of her ladies; I don't know whether they were playing comette,[2] although that game is interesting and refined, to the extent that one can hardly play anything else when one has taste—perhaps they

---

[2] *Comette*, or *comète*, was a French card game similar to the English Newmarket; all the cards in a deck were distributed to the players, who then took turn to lay down the cards, if they were able to do so, in numerical sequence—thus making a series supposedly reminiscent of a comet's tail, the player supplying the king having the right to start a new sequence with a card of his or her choice. The first player to dispose of all of his or her cards won.

did not have enough intelligence as yet to understand it fully.

When Their Majesties were served, everyone was placed, in accordance with rank, around an immense horseshoe, at the center of which were Alzopha and Brazile and on the wings, at a certain distance, their entire count and household. There was no talk of anything but pearls and oysters; that was the news of the day. They were devoured fricasseed by all hands and in all sauces; no one wanted to eat anything else; everyone was stuffed, all the way to the least servant. Irou and Alacen were the only ones who did not touch that favorite comestible; they were young lords, the most blasé in the court, who were living on milk in order to recover a good temperament that they had never had, and which no one had any desire to give them in order to lose. When the supper was over, everyone retired, moderately content with their fortune but very flattered by their hopes.

The king and the queen slept that night like the least of their subjects—which is to say, very well. They went to bed together simply and tenderly—in a word, like veritable spouses of the Golden Age. They were about to congratulate one another on the tranquility of their slumber when they alarmed to discover that they were reciprocally imperceptible.

The king was afflicted by the extreme smallness that had overtaken the queen in a single night; for her part, she was in despair at seeing the king reduced in such a short space of time to trivial dimensions. Neither of them thought, in the first moment, of being afflicted on their own account, but a brief return to themselves informed each of them that they had been equally maltreated, reduced to a height of exactly six inches, and not a whit more.

A more detailed examination offered nothing consoling: little arms, little legs and little eyes, exact and distressing in their proportions. Their Majesties were very seriously afflicted; it is even said that the king wept; as for the queen, the fact is certain.

"What will my courtiers say, some of whom are of enormous stature?" said the king, putting his little hand to his little forehead.

"Oh, Sire," replied the queen, with sobs that almost prevented her from making herself understood, "your courtiers respect you and fear you; the grandeur of sovereigns is all in their soul and her virtues; but nothing can dispense a queen of having a lovely face and an ordinary height. I'll be the fable and the laughing-stock of the coquettes and fops of your court; you know that it's full of them."

They dared not summon a single one of their servants, who slept in nearby rooms, for fear of seeing the entrance of men five-and-a-half feet tall, who would be as many insults for persons of six inches. The queen also feared more than death the first glance of her women.

What was happening in the apartment and the heart of the king was also happening throughout his court; everyone was reduced to the same degree of smallness. Everyone was desolate in consequence, and dared not emerge from their holes or show themselves. Everyone who had eaten the little oysters the day before was in the same condition.

It was noon, however, on all the repeating watches, which went like the sun; the times of the *grand* and *petit lever*, supposing that they had them, had passed. [3] Finally, Irou and Alacen were the first and the only ones who went into their master's apartment. Not daring to approach the platform on which the king and queen slept on cushions which was closed and surmounted by a kind of pointed needle, to which curtains were attached. They were about to withdraw, respectfully, when the king, who distinguished their gigantic stature through a tiny hole, shouted to them with all his might to approach. They scarcely heard him, his voice was so weak and high-pitched.

Alzopha interrogated them as to what had become of all his servants. They had not encountered anyone at their posts. They admitted to him that they had found that solitude disquieting, and that the sound of his voice, having become high-pitched in one night, augmented their alarm further.

"The strangest accident," the king said to them, "has, in fact, happened to us. The queen is inconsolable and so am I. You'll know soon enough what it's about. Don't seek to divine it before I can instruct the princes of the blood and my entire court publicly. Have all those who ought to be here, and don't have the custom of failing, come right away; their absence announces something extraordinary to me."

---

[3] The *lever* [rising] was a curious ceremony of the French court introduced and elaborated by Louis XIV, which survived into the following reign. Unlike the real sun, the Sun King rose twice, inviting a few intimates to his initial emergence from his bed—his *petit lever*—and his dressing for the day, which took a long time and required the attentions of many servants. The *grand lever* was his emergence, fully dressed, to greet his entire court. The custom is mentioned again in "The Enchanter's Mirror."

Irou and Alacen did not ask anything further; the sound of their master's voice, combined with the chagrin of the queen, caused them to imagine more than they dared to say. Irou, although he was a fop, had an excellent heart, and felt sincerely sorry for the king. As for Alacen who was ambitious and who loved the queen, he was already building hopes and chimeras on the loss by which he supposed her to be chagrined. Both of them ran where the king had ordered them to go, and soon afterwards, his apartment was full of runts and pygmies. The tallest measured six inches, but those who had been poorly built before the metamorphosis had four or five at the most; those who were hunchbacked previously had lost almost nothing of their humps; they were scarcely able to carry them, and bore more resemblance to large truffles than little humans.

Their attire further augmented the absurdity; the previous day's clothing was no longer suited to today's small stature; everyone had bundled themselves up as best they could; some were stuffed entirely into a single glove, of which they had cut off three fingers, so that the two that remained formed trousers of a sort. Others were wedged into little socks, in which they had made holes through to pass their arms; one could only see their heads.

The person whose outfit seemed the best contrived was Grifak, the Chief Justice; he was a venerable old man, well made before the common accident. His only covering was a large square wig; as he now required very little for his head, a great deal remained for his body, and, the head-gear taking on and following the forms he wanted to give it, it was attached under the throat with a crimson ribbon; his arms passed through two holes and were covered up to the elbow with the floating curls that the wig formed at that point, attached again over the breast and navel with a red ribbon. The head-dress finished there and the rest of its faces floated around, dangling to the knees; the rear curl formed a kind of trailing tail. It was thought that there was no affectation, and a good deal of taste, in that costume.

Partly consoled and emboldened by the total diminution of his court, Alzopha emerged from behind the curtains; his stature, having become perfectly similar to that of his courtiers, was a subject of acclamations and real joy for them.

It was a question of dressing him decently. A needlework-basket was presented to him; the bottom was removed, holes were made for the arms, and in no time at all it became a complete garment in very good taste. It was green and gold, very nicely embroidered in chain-stitch.

The queen held firm behind the curtains and swore not to show herself until she knew that all the kabas who were there—the equivalent of our duchesses—were appropriately tiny and proportionate to her. The most gallant lords swore that she would be content and that not one had escaped, but she wanted to see them all before making up her mind. It was terrible job to convince them to do it; every lover and husband went in search of his own, and had great difficulty in engaging or forcing her to appear. There was nothing but cries, hysteria and fainting fits every time one went past a mirror, but finally, all of them were gathered around the queen's bed, making contortions that did not magnify them by a fraction of an inch. Then she showed herself, seeing her subjects in unison.

There was a great deal of discussion regarding such a strange adventure; they agreed that there was an element of sorcery and enchantment; could anyone reasonably have thought otherwise? It remained to be determined where the coup had come from. While the politicians lost themselves in arguments and conjectures, Irou and Alacen returned; they attracted all gazes and all suspicions; they were the only ones in their natural state. People began to murmur; soon they were being accused overtly. In those savage courts, it is nothing to be convicted of certain crimes, and a great deal to be suspected of some; this one was of a nature not to be easily forgiven; there was talk of stoning them in the public square. The more moderate wanted them to be strangled in secret, courteously.

Alzopha imposed silence and made a speech full of eloquence, but furnished with little good sense, in which he did his best to prove the for and against of the little and the big, and ended up by saying that his stature of today gave him a great anxiety about the oysters of the day before, which he believed to be all the better founded when he recalled, at that moment, that Irou and Alacen had been the only ones who had not touched them.

That reflection, which he threw out at hazard, was, however, the best thing he said; the two giants recovered courage, and offered to make a proof of it immediately, even if they were to be annihilated and reduced to two inches, so true is it that a courtier will sacrifice everything to his fortune. Those offers reconciled them with the more reasonable members of the assembly; they opined that they ought to make the trial at that very moment, with the exception of one old kaba, who doubtless believed that she had acquired rights over the stature of Alacen, and would be very glad if nothing were retrenched therefrom. She was heaped with the kind of court applause that is worth as much as whistles.

Alzopha, who had longer views that any of the members of his council, also opposed it, observing that it was not merely a matter of reducing to six inches—the measure of the court—two courtiers who offered themselves to it with a good grace, but that it was necessary to take precautions and make arrangements against the people, who would gain nothing by only being six inches tall and would have nothing to lose by conserving five and a half feet, and who, for that reason, would flatly refuse to taste any oyster, instead of volunteering to do so, like Irou and Alacen; it would be impossible to engage them to do it other than by cunning.

For the honor of the king and all his court, he said, as well as the maintenance of authority, it was necessary to render the stature of his subjects almost equal, and in order to do that, to commence by ascertaining whether the diminution was due to the shellfish by making a trial in great secrecy, and after that, by making every subject in his kingdom swallow some, irrespective of age, sex or condition. He was applauded extravagantly.

It was decided that no one except for Alacen and Irou and would leave the king's hut—which can be named a palace or Louvre if you wish—and that the two lords would go on behalf of their master to announce in all the huts in his empire, where each family lived separately and distant from the others, in a similar fashion to the habitations in our Martinique, that Alzopha had resolved to share the treasures of his fishing with all his subjects, and that by rendering to the palace the following day, everyone would receive an oyster of exquisite taste and a pearl of considerable price.

While that message was being delivered, a trial was made on a few minor slaves of the king's household who had not taken part in the feast, and it was observed, with great astonishment, that after giving each of them a single oyster, as they digested it and it dissolved in their stomach, they dissolved too and diminished visibly. No one any longer doubted that the spell was in the shell-fish, and the savants of the court attributed the slowness with which the people of quality had diminished to the indolence of their stomach and the burden they had placed on it.

Preparations were therefore made for the following day's pastime. In the meantime, people employed the time in accustoming themselves to their smallness and extracting advantages from it; one can do that on a small scale as well as a large one.

Irou and Alsacen spread joy and hope in the huts of the Alzophages; each family was invited for a different time, in order to prevent confusion. They awaited the designated moment with impatience; to receive an oyster on the part of the king and to be invited on his orders—what generosity! It is not so much the gift as the fashion of giving and offering it that renders precious what the great offer us; but to that oyster was also attached a large pearl; the oyster appeared much better in advance.

While the Alzophages were nourishing themselves on that smoke, the court was disposed to receive them with pomp and dignity. Alzopha had placed himself on his throne—not the one that suited his defunct stature, where he would not have been perceived; one had been made in proportion to his new dimensions. It was a kind of coffee-table, in the middle of which he was seated, like a large sugar-bowl; around him were arranged the queen and the princesses, similar to half a dozen Dutch cups and saucers, red, blue, gold and silver. They were well-dressed; necessary provides expedients. All the dolls in the court had been stripped naked; some of them had been very dear and very well equipped. Their entire wardrobes had been requisitioned, by means of which people had decent clothes adapted to their stature. For their part, the men had dispossessed monkeys and lap-dogs that had had a few items of clothing, and cardboard marionettes. Those who had not had such resources had swathed themselves appropriately. In brief, the court was as good as it could be.

Only one family at a time was admitted to the interior of the palace; it could be composed of a hundred, or even two hundred, Alzophages; until they had been expedited, the next family was not allowed in. The order was that in the first hall they found Irou and a few slaves of previous dimension; the will and the pleasure of the king was announced to them, and anything that anyone cared to add. Then they quit a kind of simarre, or ceremonial mantle, in which they would have been embarrassed or lost as they shrank toward the complete diminution that awaited them. They were only left a kind of sheath or loincloth, in which they could wrap themselves up to the neck as they arrived at five or six inches.

The will of the king and the fashion of the court were more than enough to determine an entire people immediately. They simply quit their simarres without saying a word, and passed in their loincloths into the next hall, where they found a long table covered with the pearly oysters, very appetizing and wide open. Alacen did the honors. He had a few slaves with him, of the number that had remained tall, and who had the task of opening the oysters and preventing each of the guests from taking more than one in passing.

They each had, therefore, to take the oyster and swallow it without stopping, with the result that by marching in single file and continuing on their way through a number of other rooms, which led to the foot of the throne, they walked far enough to have the time to digest the oyster and arrive precisely, in the condition of five or six inches, at the hall where Alzopha was awaiting them. Their pearls grew as they diminished, encumbering them; each one held it in both hands, and if it fell, they fell with it, full length, but without hurting themselves—which is one of the great advantages of smallness.

However large the strides are that one takes with small legs, one is always on the road for a long time. The little Alzophages, in spite of hurrying, arrived very slowly in the presence of heir sovereign; they saw him without seeing him, along with all his court; they searched with their eyes, and had as much difficulty making themselves noticed as they did in perceiving him. Certain grimaces of chagrin or astonishment that escaped the newly diminished amused the courtiers shrunk the day before, who had already accustomed themselves to it.

Alzopha consoled his subjects by saying to them: "My children, you are sharing the fortune and disgrace of everyone that is most respectable and most noble in the court. As you can see, your sovereign is not exempt therefrom."

To others he said: "My friends, the oyster you have just eaten has produced strange marvels, but it is evident that I have eaten some, like you, and I promise you that not one of my subjects will be affranchised from it."

To some he said: "It is for the sake of order and the public good; it is because I love you, and I wanted to command and protect you always; because I wanted to bring you closer to me, in the same fashion that all those you can see have been."

At those words, all the Alzophages, who were the best people in the world, were cheered up and consoled. It is always a pleasure for the common people to share something with the aristocracy; if it is an inconvenience, an absurdity or a calamity, it does not matter; one resembles in that regard people of high status and quality; it seems that it brings them closer.

Every family came, therefore, to receive the oyster, the pearl and the little speech of consolation and the compliment from its monarch; and each one quit him shrunk, annihilated, and yet enchanted by his generosity, so true is it that a word from a king is like a hair that one loves: it pulls harder than four oxen.

As they did not want those who had not yet entered to be warned about what awaited them by seeing the form of those who emerged, they were made to pass, as they were expedited, into the interior of the palace, where there were halls and gardens that could have contained twice as many such people.

Every hut and every family had its turn; not one escaped. No one remained but Irou, Alacen and a few lowly servants; they did not have to be begged, turning the matter into a joke, guzzling oysters and shrinking with the best will in the world; after which the exit was free and everyone was the master of carrying away his pearl and his fix or six inches to his hut. No one thought about anything any longer but the general shrinkage of furniture, vehicles and clothing, and the invention of fashions proportionate to the state they were in. The matter was too serious for them to think about anything else for quite a long time.

Ladders were necessary to reach a thousand things that one could have picked up two days before without bending down. They were necessary to reach chairs, tables and beds—and what beds! One got lost in them; one spent the night searching them, and only got one's bearing at daybreak. Ladders were also necessary to descend into chests and get out of them. That was a lamentable state of affairs in the beginning. Every Alzophage went about with his little ladder in hand, as our ladies have their fans and our bourgeois their umbrellas.

A few items of furniture that served for some purpose could be employed for others; a chamber-pot quite naturally became a bathtub, for example; a little ring made a large necklace—but how many other things became useless!

While the Alzophages were occupied in repairing this disorder, thinking, as is reasonable, of the superfluous in preference to the necessary, which is always obliged to come because one cannot do without it, the Kanoris, for their part, had entirely opposite embarrassments and chagrins. Their large oysters, furnished with little pearls, had produced a contrary effect to Alzopha's. The men and women who had eaten them had grown prodigiously, with the difference that the extension took place in them slowly and gradually. The result was that they saw themselves growing every day, without knowing when it would end.

Kanor, initially ignorant of the property of the oysters, had not obliged anyone to eat them, but he had not prevented anyone from doing so, and the catch had been so abundant that all his subjects were provided with them; he had even thrown away a large number, after removing the pearls; thus, no one escaped the general aggrandizement.

The embarrassment was even greater among the latter people; the Alzophages were fixed and certain of not being able to shrink further, but for a long time the Kanoris did not know how far it might go. Someone who had been able to go in through a door the day before could not get out again when he had grown, and found himself a prisoner.

As there is nothing that does not have a measure, the Kanoris saw the end of their trouble and ceased growing after a certain time; they ended up being giants of some eight or nine feet, as their neighbors had become pygmies, and as everything is balanced in life, advantages and disadvantages are too. The small people became livelier, stronger and more adroit, and the woman became more fecund, whereas the colossi became heavier and slower in reproduction.

The two sovereigns, equally interested in clarifying the origin of their calamity, exchanged condolences and sent ambassadors. Alzopha's arrived within range of the Kanoris to whom they wanted to speak by means of the little ladders they used very adroitly; they climbed like squirrels, in the blink of an eye, all the way to the ear and shoulder of their equals, supporting the ladder gently on the stomach. With those to whom they owed respect and regard, they only climbed as far as the breast, and did not support the ladder on them, but placed it against a wall or waited for a domestic to come and take it. It was a customary politeness never to lean a ladder on any woman in order to speak to her.

The Kanoris lay down full length in order to speak to Alzophages of the highest rank; they knelt down in order to speak to those of an inferior order, and sat on the ground to converse with their equals or those to whom they did not wish to render any honors.

The politicians, doctors and scholars of the two nations were assembled—which is to say, those who believed themselves to be politicians, doctors and scholars, for it comes to the same thing in all parts of the world. They agreed, not without saying many futile things, that it was a trick of some malevolent fays hostile to the two kingdoms, but how could they divine with whom they were dealing?

Fortunately, someone remembered a costume ball at which Fierotine and Bamba, two extremely malevolent fays, had made an unpleasant scene to which no one had paid enough attention.

In order to understand the subject of those fays' annoyance, it is necessary to know that on the occasion of some celebration or other, Alzopha had given a ball for Kanor and all his court; everything that could render it brilliant was lavished there, dazzling illumination from ground level, to the vault; a rain of wax over all the costumes; utter confusion; and refreshments in such profusion that they were being trampled underfoot, for want of people knowing where to place their feet or where to walk. In a word, it only lacked space.

There had been the folly of allowing entry without tickets. In the middle of the night however, two ragged bats devoid of diamonds presented themselves; they were refused flatly. They pierced the ceiling and fell into the middle of the hall like true bats, which might have been nailed there and had detached themselves. Frightened ladies screamed and fainted; those with beautiful cleavages only came round after being unlaced. The fops, fleeing, screeching, buzzing and breaking things, finally wanted to tame then, and gradually approached the teasing, pestering bats, wanting to know who they were. One received a well-applied flick on the nose without seeing the hand that delivered it; another, wanting to lift the beard from the mask, felt the scratch of a claw. A robed Adonis, even more maltreated, felt the string of his hairpiece break, which an invisible force tore away, and the fellow who had such a beautiful head of hair instantly became decidedly bald.

People fled those masked villains; horrible things were said; someone swore that he knew them for miserable creatures who…another was sure that he had seen the little one with the cat's beard; another wanted to be dishonored if that was not **** and her companion. Finally, to put an end to the tumult, Alzopha ordered that they be asked politely to unmask and make themselves known, or to retire. Then the ladies removed the masks and revealed the visages of two fays—which is to say, ravishingly beautiful but fake, as are all their palaces. There were protestations, people wanted to give them eulogies, but it was too late; they made frightful grimaces, blew out all the candles and disappeared. Thus the ball ended.

A few days later, strange, almost effaced characters had been seen on the walls of the hall; no one had paid much attention to them then, but they were remembered now; no one doubted any longer that they were the key to the enigma. How could they be deciphered? No one could understand any of them.

They had recourse to oracles, to diviners, and to fortune-tellers; all of them understood the magical characters marvelously; they explained them very clearly, so they said—but in reality, their responses were even more obscure than the characters themselves.

Some distance away from the two kingdoms there was a witch famous for all the petty trivia that make people of that métier fashionable; she was old and ugly, only had two teeth, half outside and half inside the mouth, she was thin and dark with little red eyes; what more is necessary? She dressed in an extraordinary fashion, and only allowed herself to be seen at night, by the pale and tremulous light of a smoky little lamp; the walls of her lair were covered in poisonous herbs, baroque seashells, the hearts of bats, broomsticks, feathers and the heads of snakes—in sum, all the apparatus of the Sabbat and the finest devilry. With all that, she knew how to find things that were not lost; she announced the deaths of aged aunts in autumn, the defeat of young nieces in spring, and the ruination of pupils by tutors, and everything happened at the appointed time.

Kanor and Alzopha sent her a copy of the mysterious characters, and the obligatory presents. She received the gifts without pulling faces, but she pulled a great many before replying. Finally, in a cracked and frightening voice, in the middle of the third night, she pronounced these words:

When Kanoris for Alzophages
Burn with ardent fires,
Amour will swell little corsages
And the large will sense desires.

Kanor and Alzopha were content with the oracle and believed that they understood it. Convinced that it was sufficient to mingle the two peoples in order to repair their stature, Alzopha married a few of his runts with giant Kanori women; a few six-inch women also had the courage to marry eight-foot men, but that did not produce anything.

The little women were sterile for a long time, became bored, and made little men that the huge husbands did not want to recognize, so much did they give the appearance of having six-inch fathers. The little Alzophages fared no better with the giant Kanori women; they said astonishing things about them. When it is always necessary to have a ladder in hand to beat one's wife or to say sweet things her, one has a great deal to complain about; all that made for the worst households in the world.

They returned to the Sibyl; they made her greater presents than the first time, in order to put her in a better mood, for savage priests were very fond of money, and priestesses too. They complained that her response was false or obscure, since they had done what she had said and nothing had happened for which they had hoped. Grumbling, she made them understand that they were all idiots, to believe that amour could follow marriage, when it has so much difficulty preceding it.

She added: "Don't expect Hymen to work miracles among you that are reserved in every country for Amour alone; let your dwarf-women commence by making themselves loved; let your myrmidons learn to please, in order that they might unite afterwards, and you'll see marvels. But that's not all; it's necessary that it commences with a prince and princess of the two nations; otherwise, you won't achieve anything, and you'll all remain such as the fays and destiny have made you."

Having said that, she retired into her cavern.

The men who had been sent returned very sadly, and spread consternation by announcing that response. "What!" they said, afflicted. "It's necessary for an eight-foot prince or princess to love a six-inch princess or prince? And it has to be done without the design to marry?"

"Oh, we won't shrink!" cried the Kanori women.

"We'll never grow, alas," replied the little Alzophages. "The best-matched princes so rarely love one another when it's a matter of marriage—all the more so when it's necessary and commanded."

Alzopha, who had great sense in a little head, did not despair. He often said: "The more extraordinary and difficult things are, the more the taste of certain princes for them can be piqued. It might happen that a whim might take one of them for one of our little princesses, who might otherwise be of such great merit that her little body will be overlooked; or, one of our princes might have such big ideas that he will enchant one of those enormous princesses, compared with whom men of ordinary dimensions appear small. Those giant princesses have been known to covet little men; they must have the wherewithal to succeed on a grand scale; if they can get that far, amour and destiny will do the rest and all will be well."

For want of anything better, it was necessary to be content with those hopes.

The Alzophages, convinced that they had a long time to remain in the same condition, thought about procuring all the little commodities proportionate to six inches. All the spaniels, barbets, hounds, Great Danes and even Angolas[4] were equipped and trained in order to

---

[4] It is unclear what the author might means by "Angolas." I suspect that what he has in mind, here and in the other in-

provide mounts and beasts of burden. They were harnessed to little carts made expressly; they were trained for hunting and for war, taking care only to make use of gelded animals, because of their lack of discipline when they were not. Huts were built that resembled burrows externally, but were nevertheless clean, comfortable and even magnificent internally.

Kanor had three sons and no daughters. Alzopha also had two princes and no princesses; thus, nothing could be expected in favor of the peoples from the present state of the royal families; but Brazile, who was goodness personified, was burning with the desire to render to every one of her subjects what they had lost. She talked about nothing else except the daughters she intended to give the king, if that was his pleasure. All the charlatans who had secrets and recipes for that were welcome at her court.

Eventually, she became pregnant; her joy was extreme; that of the people was no less intense; no one dared to doubt the sex of the child to be born; the queen would have sworn to it; the physicians answered for it with their heads. All the favorite signs were there; Brazile, who did not have the full six inches, was so swollen for her height that everyone who wanted to say something nice to her assured her that she would have twins, or at least one so large that there would be no Kanori prince who could not adapt to her.

Brazile, who was about fifteen inches in circumference and five tall, counted more on the number than the height of the princesses to whom she was on the point of giving birth; the entire court was occupied in making up

---

stance where the word is used, is Angora cats, but I could be wrong.

layettes and elegant wrappings for the babies that were about to see the light of day. Bets were laid on the color of their eyes and hair.

Finally, Brazile brought into the world a very tiny boy, and the gamblers were consternated.

A year later she doubled her stake, and gave birth to another boy. The following year she doubled up again, and lost again. After that, she halved her stakes, without ever being more fortunate; it was always a boy. Finally, Alzopha accorded her all for all and no more; she lost again and the game was over.

For his part, Kanor was no more fortunate with girls; he had boys all his life.

And for several centuries, and numerous generations, only males were born in the two royal families, with the consequence that people took the same interest in the birth of a princess as they had once taken in that of a prince; the same indifference reigned for the birth of a boy as people had once had for the birth of a girl.

Finally, under the reign of an Alzopha who was the twentieth or thirtieth of that name, descending in a direct line of those eternal makers of boys, Queen Bilbaa—which, in the local language, meant "white"—became pregnant. She was the daughter of one of the principal noblemen of the court; her mother had only ever had daughters, which was a good augury, but the court's expectations had been modest in that regard for a long time; no one wagered on the outcome any longer and no one dared to make any boasts.

In the end the queen gave birth to a daughter of prodigious size for her age; she was nearly three inches. It was estimated that if she grew in proportion, she would be double the ordinary height. What joy! What hopes! She was named Babillon—which is to say, "ultimate beauty." There were public fêtes, bonfires, distributions of maize and hydromel, but so well organized that all the people were equally drunk and well nourished. The distributors were the only ones who conserved their sobriety.

The layette destined for an ordinary child, which was neatly arranged in a pill-box, could not serve Princess Babillon, the garments of a girl of fifteen were scarcely large enough for her. What a consolation, what a pleasure, for a little six-inch mother to see those things before her eyes! The king was so transported that he did not know where to put his little hands, and in his example, all the men of the court were embarrassed by theirs for some time.

To describe the cares with which the princess was brought up, all the pretty things that she was made to say and do before talking, and without thinking about it, would take forever. At the age of four years old she was as tall as the queen and already speaking Alzophage and Kanori very well—although she only had one tongue, like the majority of women, she made use of it with so much superiority and advantage that she seemed to be speaking the two jargons at once.

Since Alzopha had become a father he had put everything to work to conciliate the good graces of the hostile fays. Fierotine and Bamba had been heaped on his behalf with compliments, apologies and presents, but the wrath of fays is terrible, and the passions are strong in women who do not grow old! Fortunately, the species is rare nowadays.

Bamba, who had elongated the Kanoris, consented in good faith that they might shorten, but Fierotine, who had shortened the Alzophages, could not resolve to suffer that they be elongated. She had not been able to harm

41

their princess at the moment of her birth; her power over that people had been consummated by the malevolent action she had committed in reducing them to triviality. She therefore thought about harming them indirectly.

On the same day that Babillon was born, the Queen of the Kanoris gave birth to twin princes, perfect in their resemblance and beauty. They were heaped with all gifts and all talents by a large number of fays who were friends of their family. Fierotine did not fail to be present incognito—which is to say, invisibly, that being the best species of incognito one can maintain—and during the confusion and the chatter, which is the same everywhere, she found the opportunity to put in her word in a whisper. As she could not destroy what the other fays had done, she contented herself, unable to do any worse, with inspiring in the elder the most powerful aversion for little women, and she obtained from destiny that the talents of the younger would not develop before the age of twenty.

The two princes were brought up with extreme care; the elder, who was named Aazul—which is to say, "perfect"—succeeded in every fashion of surpassing the most exaggerated hopes; one would have said of an ordinary person that he promised a great deal, but of a prince the expression is too feeble; immediately, people cried miracle and prodigy, unable to augment it thereafter.

They had masters so expensive that it was almost impossible that they could not be good, and yet they had no success with the younger, who was named Zaaf—which is to say, "exactly similar." In truth, he appeared to have nothing in common with his brother except his facial features; apparently incapable of acting and thinking, he did not show any disposition for anything at all.

The people of the court, convinced that he was irremediably stupid, contented themselves with saying that he was a little slow; they did not think they were speaking so truthfully.

They were both unaware of the interest that he two nations had in the engagement of the elder or the younger with the princess, and the prayers they formed for that engagement to commence with a veritable amour. Babillon was no better informed. They had been deliberately maintained in that ignorance. The politics was good; there in no perfect amour that is not free; to want to give birth to it is to put an obstacle in its path.

When the princess entered her fifteenth year she was ten inches tall; nothing so grand had shone for a long time in the eyes of that people. What height! What majesty! Ten inches at fifteen years, without expectations! She appeared to them to be a colossus; they feared that so much height might give her a mannish appearance, and that she might appear too tall to the Kanori princes.

Finally, the day fixed to enable her to see the princes arrived. It began with races, combats and daces, at which Babillon appeared with all the splendor that youth, beauty, advantageous stature and adornment can provide. For their part, the princes were marvels—which is to say that Aazul was, for Prince Zaaf only did his best, and his best was the most pitiful thing in the world.

Alzopha and his entire court were arranged on an elevated amphitheater surmounted by a kind of awning made of large interlaced feathers. That elevation almost put them at the height of the Kanoris; at a distance, they rather resembled excellent marionettes to which an expert puppeteer hidden under the plumes of the awning was imparting movement without being visible.

Between his two sons, Kanor came to salute the Queen of the Alzophages and Princess Babillon, who held herself as upright as a unique daughter and as proud as a spoiled child. At close range she was all charm and grace from head to toe.

The king made the two princes a compliment full of wit and dignity.

Aazul looked at them in a distracted and advantageous manner, saluted them rather as a young marquis salutes aged noblewomen, and said a hundred pretty things to them in the most obliging fashion; he had a great deal of the wit that does not please, interrogated, made comparisons, took care not to respond appropriately, and concluded by devouring a superb collation, of which he scarcely gave Babillon time to do the honors.

As for Zaaf, he did not say a word, but he always looked at Babillon with an attention and an astonishment that she took for admiration, and his silence appeared to her to be a timid respect, with the result that, for the first time in his life, he succeeded better than his brother, without speaking, and pleased more. He perceived that, and ran the risk of becoming even more stupid; that is the effect that success produces n those who are stupid by nature, but as he was only stupid by fate, it commenced in him a first development. From the very next day onwards something nobler and more decided appeared to shine in his eyes.

The princess noticed that, and applauded herself for it; she became more beautiful and more interesting thereby. A woman perceives how a nascent amour embellishes her and the joy that she has in that renders her even more beautiful. It seems that her amour and her

44

gratitude increase with her charms; the lover who inspires that sentiment of gratitude is penetrated by it himself; the greatest obligation we can have to the object that charms us and pleases us is to charm us and please us even more. How do savages know that? They do not know it; it is amour that knows it, everywhere, and which operates within them without them knowing it; they are only more fortunate for that, because it is much better to experience the plenitude of the sentiment than it is to be able to rationalize it.

Aazul, who did not see his brother with Babillon's eyes, found it very singular that she showed his brother such marked politeness and preference. He made jokes about it and found little Babillon to have depraved tastes—for he would have been very sorry to pronounced her name without joining the quality of "little" to it, as he would have been afraid that it might have misinterpreted. That passed in Alzopha's court for a misplaced affectation in the mouth of a giant, and no one liked it. As for Zaaf, they found him the best child in the world, almost because he did not speak.

However, the fête was due to last a week, and it was only the second day; the third was destined for a concert in which the Alzophage musicians and singers performed marvels; almost all of them played instruments with the utmost perfection and usually had beautiful voices. The princess sang a very tender narrative in which she expressed an "I love you" after nature, looking very tenderly at Prince Zaaf. He was penetrated by that, to the point that a second development occurred within him. He had not been able to string together two notes in ten years of lessons, but he retained that "I love you" admirably well, he sang it accurately and he repeated it a hundred times over during the rest of the day with enough finesse and grace for a giant. He even pushed boldness and development so far as to add a sigh to it, while gazing at the princess.

Those giant sighs were forceful and indiscreet; the entire court noticed them; the princess blushed at them and was moved by them. Aazul immediately wanted to make a nasty joke about them, and said that his brother had just expressed by a sigh the regret for the silence that the princess had caused him to break.

Babillon, piqued, said to him: "Prince, I believe that I would oblige you both if I engaged him to say a little more and you much less."

Aazul's only response was an acidic smile.

The following day's pleasure were to commence with a ring race, in which Babillon prepared to make the princes see her skill and grace in handling an extremely spirited barbet gelding as black as jet. It was equipped in the richest and most gallant fashion, like all those that were to serve as mounts for the Alzophage ladies.

When the signal was given, Babillon leapt on to her barbet lightly and gracefully and made it prance a few times. Taking in hand a small lance of light gilded wood, she departed like an arrow, extending her arm ready to catch the ring that was attached to a stake a hundred paces away. She was followed by a few ladies of the court, who were not mounted as advantageously as her and were not as able as she was to govern their mounts.

As she approached the stake, it was remarked that the princess's barbet was veering away, as if in spite of her; soon it was perceived that it was carrying her away at an extreme speed, like an impetuous horse that has taken the bit between its teeth and whose rider can no longer retain it.

Alzopha, the queen and all the Alzophage people uttered loud cries on seeing Babillon and the barbet about to plunge into a dense forest full of wild beasts, which none of them had dared to enter since their reduction to six inches, for fear of being devoured.

Kanor and his courtiers watched that caprice and that canine abduction with astonishment, but none took upon themselves to fly to the princess's aid, even though they were capable of overtaking the abductor. Zaaf was the only one who, without any other weapon than a bow and arrows, and without consulting any other impulsion than that of his heart, launched himself after the barbet like lightning.

He was on foot, but amour and long legs travel very rapidly. Aazul and a dozen courtiers, who had commenced by deliberating for a long time and making many futile remarks before following him, ran after him quite uselessly, as fast as they could; they could not catch up with him. They saw him enter the forest almost on the heels of the enraged barbet that was carrying his lover away—one can give that name in advance to the unfortunate Babillon, for from that moment on, she became seriously entitled to it.

The misfortune of a lovely woman is so appropriate to complete making her beloved when the work has been commenced in a period of calm! An unfortunate young woman for her part, has so much disposition to deliver herself entirely, during the misfortune, to a penchant born in days of prosperity!

Aazul and those who were following him searched in vain for Zaaf, the princess and the barbet throughout the forest; they made it resound in vain with the names of Babillon and Zaaf far into the night; their strides and their cries were wasted; they did not perceive the slightest trace of them, and came back in a very ill humor to give that bad news to people who were already consternated, and whose despair was completed by their return.

You might become anxious for the prince and the princess if we deferred any longer saying what had become of them.

First of all, the black barbet was none other than the malevolent Fierotine; she had got rid of the princess's veritable mount, either by changing it into a ant or a flea, with a few words appropriate to that purpose, or with a single tap of her wand, and she had established herself in its skin.

Zaaf, not thinking about a fay, still having the dog and the princess in sight, ran to the point of collapse, always ten feet from the barbet, always about to put his hand on it, so he thought. Finally, when he felt that his strength was almost exhausted and he was on the point of succumbing, he gathered everything for one last effort, and made a leap so prodigious that he fell, but so fortunately and so accurately that he did so on the princess and the dog.

He would inevitably had stifled Babillon, in view of the weight quite natural to large bodies and the force of the fall, if the princess had not found herself, by the greatest good fortune, caught sideways between his breast and his chin, which settled on the ground and left sufficient room to accommodate, without too much inconvenience, a princess about four or five inches in girth.

As for the wretched dog, which was trapped under his abdomen, it was flattened like a sole, and it was as well that it was a fay and not a simple barbet, or it would never have recovered.

Caught between the chin and the neck of her lover, Babillon had fainted; a princess so well brought up never fails to do that on essential occasions.

Zaaf, not having the strength to get up again, and being out of breath to the point of needing half a hour to get it back, moved his head in order not to leave the princess in a vice, in such a fashion that his huge face found itself close to the little miniature that Babillon's formed. He perceived that she was no longer breathing; he uttered a terrible and dolorous cry, and, moving even closer, he could not retain a profound sigh, which departed from the seizure and tenderness of his heart.

That burning breath appeared to reanimate his lover and render her life; her eyes opened slightly, and in her turn, she sighed, so justly, that the little breath that departed from her heart mingled and was confounded with a second sigh, all fire, that the charm of finding her alive drew from the prince's soul.

Those disproportionate breaths were united, almost as a light vapor, as the gentlest zephyr might be united with an impetuous whirlwind. It was precisely that union, that mixture, that was the decisive talisman. It was on the reiterated repetition of these mingled and confused sighs that the entire development of the prince's mind, the diminution of his height and the increase of that of the princess depended.

How could they have divined it? They could only owe those miracles to hazard. Fortunately, they were well placed for those hazards to be repeated frequently. Having come round completely, Babillon said, while sighing again: "Oh, Prince, where are we? By virtue of what strange adventure do I find myself in your arms, in a country that is unfamiliar to me?"

Zaaf would probably have been embarrassed by those questions an hour before, but Babillon's little breath had dissipated a part of the charm. He took one of her hands, which he kissed tenderly, and rendered her an account of the stampede of the barbet, his pursuit, the race and the fall that he had made. He added, in a tone that had not the slightest hint of the ogre about it: "How I am repaid for it, utterly charming princess, since my eyes see you again, since my mouth…."

He did not finish, and seemed to want to be repaid again.

"Get up, dear prince," Babillon said to him, drawing away from him slightly. "We can't remain here for an instant without being culpable of the consternation that the Kings of Alzophagia and the Kanoris are in, regarding your loss and mine. Let's hasten to rejoin them."

If the prince owed to the accord and the mixture of his sighs with those of the princess all the intelligence that he had just caused to appear, the princess had no less obligation to them; she had grown by four inches. Another advantage was that, the talisman of union having operated once, the fay could no longer subject them to all the great evils that she had projected; her power was limited to a little petty black malice, which she took care not to spare them.

She was placed near Zaaf's belt, like an old bearskin muff; we would have got her out of there sooner if it were not the case that there is no great harm in allowing the malevolent to suffer a little. If the prince had known that he had his most mortal enemy in his power, the person to whom he owed entire years of stupidity and Babillon her smallness, he would not have let her off so cheaply; for as long as he was holding her and touching her, she would have been impotent to take another form, and would have remained a flattened barbet for as many centuries as he wished, and nothing more; but he was unable to divine all those marvels. He mistook her for one of the ordinary mounts of the king's stable, thought her quite dead, and for that reason, good to leave in place.

Scarcely had he got up than she disappeared, as if she had sunk into the ground, which frightened the prince and the princess more than a little. However, it was necessary for them to make the decision to wander at random through the wood in order to find a path that might enable them to get out of it or take them to a few habitations, supposing that there were any nearby. The night was becoming darker.

Although she had grown four inches, Babillon was not in a condition to follow the giant through the brambles and the thorns. She had the resource of allowing herself to be carried. She made difficulties in that regard, but what was the point, when it was impossible to do otherwise?

Zaaf said to her everything that the circumstance gave him the right to say, and said it well; she was charmed to hear him, in spite of the obscurity of the night. People who do not talk are doubly seductive when they begin to talk well. Finally, it was with the consent of the princess that Zaaf took her in his arms and started walking.

That situation, so new for her, cost her a small sigh of anxiety and emotion; the prince responded to it with another of contentment and pleasure, and those sighs were fortunate; the same instant made them blossom; the intelligence of the prince and the height of the princess were augmented. He was not carrying her far from his face, as can be imagined; he had enough intelligence to sense the need of having doing more. Without knowing why, or how, that proximity could contribute, it seemed that he had a presentiment of it; he often changed position in order that she would be less uncomfortable; it was always with respect and decency, and it was not without saying very tender things, without sighing, or without her responding frequently, or even without them sometimes interrogating one another in the same language. But not all those sighs took effect; some of them were wasted for want of encountering one another.

They had already walked for a long way and had not found any issue. Zaaf was weakened by fatigue and need; while walking he had collected a few wild fruits; hazard enable him to encounter a steam and he proposed to the princess that they rest for a while in order to take a little nourishment. She consented to that, her lover having need of it, and in a wood, in the horror of the night, that lover was very necessary to her.

They had one of those meals of which amour and appetite make the delights; one of those meals that one is very glad to have had once in one's life, if only for the charm of remembering it. When amour is born, all is mystery; as it increases, all is confidence.

In conversing with the prince, Babillon admitted to him that she found that she had grown considerably, and she did not know whether it was due to the fright she had had or to the pleasure that had succeeded it when she had perceived that she owed her life to Zaaf. I have no doubt that she blushed as she pronounced those last words; a blush is a necessary accompaniment to the semi-declarations that a well born princess makes, as well as the overt declarations that she allows herself to make.

For his part, the prince admitted that he believed that he had more intelligence since the moment when he had found her than he had had in all the moments that had preceded it, and that he did not believe that he owed that to fear; in order to make it evident that he was not mistaken, he added, tenderly: "We owe everything to pleasure, my dear princess; we owe the happiness of our lives to it."

Those last words were accompanied by a sigh so tender that Babillon would have had no soul if she had not been moved by it and if she had not responded to it. She responded to it so justly and so well that she grew another four inches. Zaaf also sensed his intelligence and his talents developing, and remained firmly convinced that only the pleasure of being loved had brought him to the degree of improvement that he had reached.

They continued walking for a few more hours, but Zaaf sensed clearly that he was lost and that it was necessary to wait for daylight in order to reconnoiter and not to plunge any deeper into an immense forest, the extent and the routes of which he did not know. He proposed to the princess to spend the rest of the night in the first comfortable place they found.

She was extremely reluctant to do that, but it was necessary to consent to it. She was being carried very comfortably in the prince's arms but he had no relief; he had to battle continually against stones and branches. She only made him swear on the faith of a prince that he would not lack the respect that was due to her; he swore it, and she was tranquil. The slightest oath is, for savages, an inviolable and sacred guarantee of their word; that is what distinguishes them most from civilized peoples,

When Zaaf had found an appropriate place to set the princess down safely, he constructed for her, in no time at all, a bed of tender grass and moss. He strewed a few flowers over it, which he had collected near the little stream, and placed her gently on that little throne. The oath was reiterated again, and the princess went to sleep tranquilly, in complete security.

Zaaf had only obtained one of her little hands, with which he contented himself; he spent the night kissing it and watching over, in order to be able to defend, if necessary, an object that was becoming dearer to him with every passing moment.

The sun had not yet risen when Babillon opened her eyes, but there was enough light for her to glimpse her lover and the air of languor and weariness that fatigue, insomnia and passion had given him, which rendered him more redoubtable and more lovable at the same time.

He was still holding Babillon's hand; he had not perceived her awakening; he was gazing at that little hand, talking to it and kissing it in a pensive and tender fashion. She wanted to withdraw it, but she did not have the strength. The oath reassured her, but it had only been made for the night; it expired with the daylight. She admired in silence the art with which the prince had constructed, in the dark and so rapidly, the bed on which she had reposed so well. She gave him credit for everything: the softness and the freshness of the grass, the perfume and the color of the flowers; she related everything to him and found intelligence and gallantry in all of it.

Alerted by the nascent daylight to contemplate his lover, Zaaf raised his eyes toward her; on perceiving her own open and occupied in looking at him, he lowered them in a disconcerted manner, but it was only to raise he again a moment later, in such a fashion as to show them more tender and more animate. The princess's were troubled and lowered in their turn; a charming blush covered their faces; that was certainly a moment to sigh in unison, and they did not fail to do so, more than once.

They maintained silence for a few moments; finally, Zaaf broke it, and pronounced a few poorly articulated and incoherent words, which depicted the disorder and sincere passion of his soul better than the studied and flowery speeches of our seducers are able to do.

"Prince," Babillon said to him, "you need rest. Entrust your bow and arrows to me, and I will render you, for a few hours of the day, the service that you have rendered me during the night. I will defend you during your sleep; if any enemy arrives too powerful for me, I'll wake you up in order to defend me."

"My repose," Zaaf said to her, "does not depend on sleep; it depends on you, on your heart; I owe to you knowledge and sentiments of which I have only made use in order to love you. It is the only purpose to which I shall devote them; augment the treasures and possessions that are consecrated to you; it is to the innocent admixture of our souls, to the communication of your breath and mine, that I attribute the change that has taken place in me; it is to that intimate union that you owe the prompt increase in height that appears to me to have doubled in one night. I'm certain of not being mistaken."

Babillon tried to extract herself from the excess of emotion into which he had plunged her by cheerfully sustaining the contrary; they disputed the yeas and the nays for a few moments. When lovers argue, it is always without bitterness.

"I'll cede to you if you wish," Zaaf said to her, "but why remain uncertain of what could enlighten us in a moment? Suffer that I approach my mouth close enough to yours to be able to collect the divine breath to which I believe I owe everything. If that communication, even more intimate than that we owed yesterday to hazard, produces the same effect in us; if it gives you growth and me intelligence, we will know to what we owe ir. If the trial adds nothing to your height and my conceptions, we shall await the first fear to see whether it will produce more."

There was so much justice and reason in all that, that Babillon did not know how to respond. Perhaps curiosity engaged her as much as amour not to refuse the experiment. Zaaf took her silence for the watchword; a little sound of a few leaves that she heard stirring gave her a distraction and prevented her from retiring as promptly as the prince approached, with the result that neither one of them had any more doubt. A double sigh, of which nothing was lost, enabled the princess to grow six inches in an instant.

Her lover appeared to her less prodigious, and considerably more lovable, either because he had diminished, or because, as she had grown toward his height, it seemed reduced to her. There still remained a long way to go, but the princess, who did not want to fatigue her lover in becoming heavier, refused absolutely to grow and further.

He obeyed, and they resumed their march. They walked all day, much further than they had done the previous day, but were no more successful in their search: no beaten paths, no issues. The wretched fay whom they had spared led them astray and caused them to wander at random.

They spent a whole week in that fashion, nourishing themselves on fruits and roots or a few pieces of game that Zaaf killed and roasted over a fire of dry branches, which he lit by striking stones together.

As Babillon's bed was always made by her lover's hands, and he did not wait until nightfall to make it, it was always a masterpiece of savage artistry and gallant artistry, The moment of going to bed occasioned sighs of dolor; they were about to stop talking and lose sight of one another; the moment of awakening produced the joy and transport of seeing one another again. Among those surges of the heart there were always some that formed the most perfect union.

Zaaf doubted that there could be any other means for him to acquire, in an instant, all possible knowledge, and for the princess to acquire a convenient height. In that regard he had desires and anxieties that he could not conceive; he attributed that defect of enlightenment to his lack of intelligence. For her part, the princess had none of those ideas, she stuck to what hazard had allowed her to discover and imagined nothing further. That gift of hazard nevertheless led her gradually and insensibly to a height of three and a half feet by the end of the week. Zaaf had diminished almost as much as the princess had grown.

The wood in which the lovers were so thoroughly lost was full of Kanoris who were searching for them, with Prince Aazul at their head; the king had sent him into the wood with an elite troop, and precise orders not to return until he had news of his brother. The Alzophages were also searching for their princess; they were experienced and marched with a short stride in large troops, but how could they have found the couple, whom Fierotine kept hidden in a dense fog? Is there any lack of that when one is a fay, and a malevolent fay?

The wood resounded in vain with the names of Babillon and Zaaf; they were as many wasted clamors and sounds. The fog that prevented them from seeing also prevented them from hearing, and that did not cost Fierotine any more than deflecting the course of a river, exciting a tempest, constructing a superb palace in an instant, and other little tricks of the same species.

She took care not to forget the resource of an enchanted palace; she offered one to Aazul's eyes at a moment when he strayed way from his men. The prince was dazzled by it: so much architectural order, taste and magnificence, and everything that ensued, impressed him; those ladies built no others when it is a matter of setting traps for princes.

One can easily believe that Aazul went in; natural impulse dictated that; besides which, when one is at the doors of those enchanted palaces, there is always a magical force that pushes you inside. It is understandable that he traversed, without encountering anyone, great vestibules, very ornate drawing rooms, and that, passing from room to room, he traveled through a sequences of apartment each more richly and better furnished than the last, always admiring them and seeking the master of so much wealth, or someone who of whom he could ask his name. All that cannot happen otherwise.

Finally, the last room arrived, the door of which was closed; he opened it slowly and as struck by a surprise more forceful and more agreeable than all the previous ones: the sight of a young woman of an utterly divine beauty, who was sprawling on cushions—or, if you prefer, sunk into a sofa making a golden embroidery heightened by pearl and diamonds of admirable taste.

Aazul saluted her, trembling; she made him a sign to approach, saying to him: "It's Aazul, who is searching for me, and who does not recognize me."

The prince, even more astonished on hearing himself named than he had been a moment bore, lost all composure and could not recover one of those advantageous airs so necessary to a first conversation. Fierotine had taken on the entire form of Babillon: not the Babillon ten inches tall but the princess such as she was since amour had taken her in hand. So, everything was there: three and a half feet of height, the slightest of whose movements seeming to express that it was a very recent gift of Amour himself, in whom nothing remained but that; graces that a tender languor rendered even more touching; innocence and voluptuousness in every feature. It was Babillon herself, very different from the way she had appeared to the prince when she was only ten inches tall, and yet the resemblance was so close that it was impossible for him not to recognize her. It was an exquisite copy of a miniature rendered on a larger scale by a grandmaster.

Once one has taken the resemblance of someone, the hardest part is done; it is very easy to take her name. The fay did not fail to do so, and immediately, Aazul was fully convinced; what had dazzled him at first developed in his eyes; he recognized perfectly all the features of the princess. Although he had been untouched by them in miniature, on a large scale, they had all the effect that they could have.

The intention of the fay in disguising herself thus was doubly evil.

It is said in the land that when she had disguised herself as a barbet in order to abduct the princess, having been held in hand for a long time by a very short and very ugly Alzophage groom who was waiting with a number of other grooms for other barbets, which the ladies who were to compete in the ring-race had requested as their mounts, the fay, having nothing better to do, and to distract herself from the sight of the ugly groom, had amused herself contemplating the Kanori princes very attentively every time they went past the equipages. It is also said that the prince had dismounted from his horse, and, believing that he was only with grooms and barbets, had briefly taken off the loincloth that is the unique garment of those people—and the barbet had assuredly not turned its gaze away. It requires no more for a fay to covet a giant.

Now, a covetous fay does not listen to reason. If she had been content to attract the prince into her palace, if she had received him on cushions or on a sofa, it would be of no importance; those ladies have no great account to render in their procedures; but in taking the face and the name of Babillon there was the intention of a consummate rascality. The malevolent individual knew that the moment marked by destiny had arrived, that ruses could no longer delay it, and that her power over a prince and princess whom amour has united was about to end. She wanted to throw trouble into the two courts, to put uncertainty and jealousy into the hearts of the two brothers, and to dishonor Babillon even in her own eyes. To succeed in that, this is how she continued to act.

One can imagine that Aazul had an extreme urgency to know by virtue of what adventure the fay, whom he mistook for Princess Babillon, had grown so prodigiously since her flight with the black barbet. Fierotine was in no less of a hurry to inform him, in her fashion. She commenced, therefore, by making him sit down on the sofa, with all the enticements of a true coquette: little smiles and petty distraction. How could a fifteen-year-old savage defend himself? One of our thirty-year-old fops would have been duped.

She told him that when her barbet had been carried away, without her knowing the cause, she had been frightened for a long time, without losing her composure, but that in the end, the excessive movement or the fear had made her fall in a faint in the same forest where this palace was constructed. When she had recovered her senses, she had found herself in the arms of Zaaf, whose burning breath had rendered her life. For a week, he had guided her and carried her through the wood; that those travels, those fears and a few of Zaaf's sighs, mingled with hers in spite of her, had apparently caused her to grow. She had added, blushing—a fay's blush, more fake than carmine: "Zaaf, in obliging me, was serving an ingrate; my heart, in spite of me, desired to owe so many cares to Prince Aazul."

That story was not told without being interrupted many times by many rather urgent caresses on the part of the prince. The fay did not defend herself against them at all urgently. The unfortunate Aazul was inflamed very sincerely for Princess Babillon; that amour even caused his own misfortune, and preserved the true lovers, as we shall see in due course.

The more the prince's amour augmented, the more he seemed to lose the vivacity and the brilliance of his intelligence; whereas his brother had acquired more of both as his amour had augmented. It seems that the passion in question causes those who have intelligence to lose it, and gives it to those who have not.

Aazul's intelligence mattered little to Fierotine; she loved his stature, his face, his youth and nothing more; there are still Fierotines in the world.

The evil fay told the prince that in a moment when Zaaf had gone away to collect a few fruits, of which they made their nourishment, she had taken a few steps into the wood herself and had suddenly perceived the enchanted palace. She had retraced her steps in order to inform Zaaf, and having waited for him called to him and searched for him in vain, for a long time, she had finally approached the edifice, which she believed to be inhabited. She had entered it and gone through all the rooms, and had found them empty. When she had uttered a rather profound sigh, however, little men and little women had come running, of the stature of Alzophages, who had served her and who had come running whenever she sighed.

As she finished speaking she uttered one of the sighs that summoned the little men, and a magnificently served collation immediately appeared. The prince had need of it, as the fay suspected; he ate like a student—which is to say, avidly: fruits, wines, sugared pastries; nothing was spared. Fierotine was delighted by her lover's appetite, not like a young princess of fifteen, but like an old stager of a fay, who draws consequences from everything.

When the meal was over the table and the myrmidons disappeared; the conversation, and the sighs that did not summon anyone recommenced.

It is necessary now to know two things. The first is that among those peoples, marriages are either made with great ceremony, or with none at all. Those formed by politics, reasons of interest and family, demand endless preparations and arrangements. What is convenient about is that when politics, reason of interest and family cease to apply, they can be broken, and that is done immediately, without any ceremony; with the consequence that, if they take a long time to make, they are soon broken, which makes them fashionable.

The other species of marriage, made by amour alone, has no need of anything except amour: not the slightest preparation, and not the smallest ceremony. When two savages love one another, are certain of it and can prove it, the marriage is made; it is as solid and as good as the other, in their religion and in their law; but if it is a matter of breaking it, it is necessary to observe endless formalities and ceremonies. Those good people, who have no tincture of our fashions, cannot believe that one can cease to love when one has commenced. They expect people either never to love one another, or to love one another forever—which renders marriages of the second kind rarer.

The other thing that it is important to say there is that Fierotine had taken care to place before Zaaf and the princess a second palace exactly similar to the one of which mention had just been made; in order that they would enter it at the same moment when she was with Aazul in the other.

Her measures were taken in such a fashion that Babillon perceived the palace at a moment when Zaaf had quit her. After having considered for some time the structure of such a superb building, so singularly placed, she returned to the place from which she had departed, and where she expected to find the prince. After having called to him and waited in vain for a long time, despair and dread assailed her; a ferocious beast that she perceived caused her to flee toward the palace that she had just discovered.

She plunged into it as into a refuge where she hoped to find aid while awaiting her lover's return, and her fear only changed its object when, after passing through a large number of apartments, she saw an equal solitude in all of them.

She was in horror and perplexity when that palace was presented to the prince, alarmed by the loss of his lover. The hope of finding her there, or of learning news of her, rather than any impulse of curiosity, caused him to enter it.

It is a waste of effort to display gold, brocade and rubies before the eyes of a lover who has lost the person he loves and who is searching for her. He does not see any of it.

The next scene was a repetition of the one that was happening at the same moment in the other palace between Aazul and Fierotine; she had six reasons for wanting the two palaces, the two brothers and the two princesses they found therein to be in an exactly parallel situation, and that each of the scenes should depend n the other.

People who, after having lost for several hours a mistress or a lover passionately beloved, have had the good fortune to rediscover that dear object, anxious and tearful, will know the rest: everything that passed through the heart and through the eyes of Babillon and Zaaf, when they found one another again. What a lovely disorder in speech! What an enchanting disturbance in the senses! Those who know those charms can imagine everything that cannot be said; it would be cold and futile to try to depict them for others.

At the sight of the prince, Babillon fell backwards, and might have hurt herself, for her stature was beginning to reach a height that renders such falls dangerous; fortunately, a nearby settee received her.

Scarcely had she sat down on it than Zaaf was at her knees; he clasped them tenderly; his mouth expressed nothing, but his eyes watered his lover's hands with tears; joy and dolor were distinct and confounded in his gaze and in his every action; nothing says more than such a silence; the proof that it says it well is that it is understood marvelously by those to whom it is addressed. Babillon felt all its energy, to the point of only being able to respond in the same manner; that is also the best of all.

Those poor children, too emotional for having been silent for such a long time, too distressed to have the strength to speak so soon, were in a violent and awkward situation; by dint of being interesting and gentle, Amour alone broke that silence for them; he enabled them to remember that there was in their mores a marriage that had no need of anyone but him, and which only consisted in the assurance and the proof of the most tender and the most reciprocal passion, given and received.

Both of them, simultaneously enlightened and confused by that idea, communicated it one another; faith was instantly sworn, and in consequence, the marriage was celebrated; the amour that united them completed its work. It instructed them of the most profound mysteries.

That god, who protected them quite differently from vulgar lovers, had covered them with his wings and held them hidden in a cloud. Apparently, he had foreseen that Babillon would utter a few sighs, and that those sighs would summon the little hobgoblins disguised as Alzophages; charged with serving the collation. He did not want their eyes to soil a pure sensual pleasure, of which he alone was the author, and of which he wanted to be the only witness. He also was able to learn the particularities of what happened beneath his cloud; he has not informed me of them, so those who want greater detail will have to address themselves to him.

The princess did not fail to sigh many times, and the little monkeys came running, with baskets laden with fruit and especially with preserves; they had plenty of time to arrange them and serve them.

Fierotine copied the same things in her palace and on her sofa, under the face and name of Babillon; she proposed a marriage there to Aazul, to whom the idea had not yet occurred, although he was smitten with the face and the charms of which the fay only had the shadow. The marriage was celebrated; the fay parodied the sighs of the princess, as well as Amour's cloud, but doubtless one was a beneficent and light vapor and the other a black and unhealthy smoke.

That cloud of amour, which enveloped Babillon and her lover, eventually dissipated gradually, and allowed the fortunate Zaaf to see his lover embellished and grown to a point of perfection that left nothing to be desired. Her complexion had the brilliant colors, the pure and vivid incarnadine, of youth and of innocence, compounded with those of passion, and the voluptuousness of her stature had all the proportion and majesty that combined with grace.

Zaaf had also lost in the arms of amour what his stature had of the excessive and gigantic; he only retained the proportions that make an accomplished man, those of which he had need in order to appear worthy of the masterpiece that Amour had taken pleasure in perfecting.

What joy they had in seeing one another so perfect and so well matched! How tenderly they expressed themselves! Zaaf put so much into the testimony of his own that the princess hardly dared to respond, so fearful was she of the consequences. She was afraid that she might grow further, and pass, in very little time, from the stature of the smallest dwarfs to that of the most enormous giants. But the prince would not hear any argument; he had no fear of shrinking any further; he felt fixed at a point at which he was content and from which nothing could remove him.

He was confirmed in his idea by a large number of experiments by which the collation was followed, and even interrupted; Babillon knew to that her height was no longer running any risks, and that discovery augmented her confidence.

You will not have doubted that Fierotine, in order to render the imitation more perfect, had not failed to grow in Aazul's eyes at the same time, and in the same fashion, as the princess. Without knowing the art she had employed in that, however, one can assume that the operation had not been the same; Nature only ever allows herself to be imitated in a mechanical and imperfect fashion.

Doubtless the fay, in Aazul's arms, grew as one sees statues grow that are moved by springs; they rise up and develop, but it is by degrees and in equal and marked phases, in such a way that one can recognize the movement of a machine. For Babillon, her growth, determined and produced by Nature herself, had combined the economy and charm of her productions.

A flower that the morning dew and the first rays of the sun urge to bloom, develops its treasures in a equally prompt and insensible fashion; it does not hide and is not perceived; the vine extends its branches and elevates its buds when the burning midday sun penetrates it; their progress is striking and certain, but the watchful eye cannot seize it on the march.

There was a more singular difference between the two adventures, which is that Aazul remained a giant; all the fay's art could not put him at the level of his brother; destiny had only promised to render equal lovers who were united by the most sincere and the most reciprocal amour. Aazul believed that he loved a young princess in an old fay; the old fay believed that she loved the young prince, but only loved pleasure; in consequence, there was nothing reciprocal or true in their sentiments.

When Fierotine was firmly convinced that Prince Aazul was as smitten with Babillon as he could be, and that the passion in question, of which she had wanted to take advantage under the features of the princess, could not produce anything more of which she could continue to take advantage under that borrowed name, she thought that it was time to disappear.

Seizing a moment when Aazul was drowsy, she changed form and passed into the palace where Zaaf and his lover had sworn an ardor as long as life. She struck them with her wand, which was as invisible as she was, and plunged them both into a profound slumber.

The palaces, the furniture and the dwarfs that served there, all disappeared; the wood resumed its place, and in that wood, a bed of grass, on which the princess found herself placed when she awoke, a few paces from where the fay had made the two brothers profoundly torpid.

Equally astonished by the change of objects that struck her sight and no longer seeing her dear Zaaf by her side, Babillon called out in a tender and dolorous tone. That dear voice awoke the two princes at the same time, equally astonished to see one another. They both ran to the princess.

One can imagine the extreme surprise of those three individuals; a thousand different movements expressed it simultaneously; curiosity, anxiety and jealousy were born in the hearts of the two bothers. Each of them, equally certain that they had gone to sleep in a palace where they were alone with Babillon, found the absence of the palace as strange as the appearance of a third party who had had no part in his adventure.

The princess was as sad as she was alarmed by the unexpected return of her giant brother-in-law; she read in his first glance a passion that that prince believed to be very agreeable and fully authorized, and which was extremely displeasing. Zaaf, who remarked it as soon as the princess, was even more discontented and offended by it than she was.

Aazul took the cold expression of the princess for a very unwarranted caprice, given the terms that he believed himself to be on with her, and he found conceit in the jealous expression of his brother, with the consequence that before saying a word, the three individuals were already in a bad mood and rather ill disposed to one another.

Evidently, some awkward explanations would have followed rapidly, but they did not have the time; the fay who had kept them hidden until then, allowed them to be seen, and the wood was full of their subjects, occupied in searching for them. In no time at all they were surrounded, and as if assailed, by different platoons of searchers, who all came together at once and never ceased making acclamations of joy and astonishment on seeing the princess and Zaaf. It was therefore impossible for the two princes to interrogate one another and explain themselves to one another; they could not do anything except receive compliments, which annoyed them greatly, and respond to them.

I have forgotten to say two necessary things. One is that, to the extent that Zaaf had acquired intelligence in the arms of the princess, his brother seemed to have lost it in those of the fay, with the consequence that the Kanoris mistook the elder for the younger and the latter for his brother. As the resemblance between them had always been a subject of error for all those who saw them, if they had traded names, Zaaf would have been generally recognized for the elder full of intelligence and charm, Aazul for his stupid younger brother.

The other essential thing is that Babillon, who had entered the woods with clothes appropriate to a person ten inches tall, would have emerged as naked as a hand if she had not changed them, when she was five and a half feet tall; that would at least have caused talk, as anyone might suppose, and it would not have taken anything more to damage a stainless reputation.

So long as Babillon was wandering in the wood, carried by Zaaf, she had conserved all her ten-inch garments even though, in the end, she was three and a half feet tall. In truth, she suffered a great deal from that at times; nothing fit, everything was too small, too tight and too short; it was always at the expense of a few of her charms that she veiled another, but on the other hand, there was no means of doing better. In any case, there were no witnesses except for the eyes of her lover, and those eyes did not pay much attention to her garments.

By way of compensation, once she had set foot in the enchanted palace, made by the hand of a fay, she found a rich and well-matched wardrobe there; as everyone knows, fays never built palaces without wardrobes and bathrooms; they are the fundamental rooms of those edifices, as cellars and kitchens are in bourgeois houses.

The princess had taken advantage of it, as any woman would have done; and she was able to appear in the eyes of her subjects dressed in a rich and decent fashion.

Without having had the time to talk to one another, Babillon and the princes resumed the road to their estates, in the midst of a crowd of people and courtiers. It was no longer a barbet that the princess required; she mounted a superb horse, lent to her by a Kanori lord, who took one from one of his men. The princes, and everyone distinguished who was in the wood, accompanied her.

Zaaf was applauding himself in secret for possessing the heart and being the husband of such an accomplished princess; that sentiment was visible in his face. Aazul, believing her to be the same as the fay, found her even more beautiful, and he was even more amorous. Convinced that he was her husband, he believed himself less beloved since she had seen his brother. He hated him furiously, and that was expressed in his gaze; Babillon only appeared more indignant against him in consequence, and more tender toward Zaaf.

They arrived in those dispositions in Alzopha's court. Renown had preceded them and had assembled there the two kings and all the most considerable individuals in the two kingdoms. The embraces, the tears and the cries of joy were not forgotten; people looked at looked at one another for a long time without seeing, and interrogated one another without hearing or responding.

Seeing his daughter so well grown, Alzopha wanted to learn the details from her and without witnesses. He sat down on Babillon's right shoulder, and the queen sat on her left shoulder, in order that both would be able to hear her. Thus placed, they passed from the hall where the crowd was into a garden, where, out of respect, they were only followed at a distance.

Kanor, between his two sons, took another pathway; he also wanted to talk to them in private about the adventures of their journey and the present difference in their stature; it was a matter of knowing whether Zaaf had gained or lost, and how the prodigy had occurred.

The princess told her dear parents, point by point, about all the obligations she had to Prince Zaaf; she did not go into such exact detail about all the evidence she had given of her gratitude. Their Majesties wept with tenderness and joy on hearing how that generous defender had almost stifled the enraged barbet that had carried away their unique daughter, no one know where, how he had held her in his arms for entire day to defend her from thorns, how he had guarded her against wolves by night, and so many other small cares, of which she did not forget one—except for the principal care, about which she did not say a word.

Alzopha, who knew by virtue of the oracle's response the condition on which his daughter ought to grow, could not doubt that the condition had been accomplished; he told her his sentiment; she admitted everything: the palace, the settee, the collation served by dwarfs, the marriage, the prince's caresses and the passion that they had inspired in one another.

If those dear confidants had been placed elsewhere than on the shoulders of the princess she would have thrown herself at their knees in making that confession; she was too well-born to fail in that. They would have lifted her up, embracing her, for they were too tender to do otherwise, but, in order not to be out of place, the king thanked his daughter for that ceremony. The queen also acquitted her for the same reason; they both embraced her and recommended shedding tears of joy.

Alzopha told her that in loving the prince she had accomplished the decrees of destiny and the wishes of the nation, the horrible smallness of which would cease by virtue of that marriage. Babillon, charmed that the most agreeable action that she had performed in her life had been so useful to her people, was burning with impatience to share her joy with her husband; to tell him that her choice had been approved by those on whom she depended; and to present him to them under the sweet name of husband; and to hear all the flattering things that would not fail to be said on either side.

She marched with long strides toward Kanor, who had retired with his sons into an arbor. The noise that was being made there stopped her from going in. The princes were arguing heatedly. Kanor was trying to impose silence but could not succeed in doing so.

The princess wanted to know the subject of their dispute before appearing; she listened attentively through the leaves, still having the king and the queen on her shoulders, who were also listening. All three of them heard that Zaaf had married their daughter; he swore it by the Sun, an oath those peoples never took in vain. But Aazul made the same oath, and swore by all the stars.

Kanor made them repeat the circumstances; they were the same; he was lost therein: the same palace, the same height of three and a half feet in the princess before the marriage, the same growth thereafter; the same dwarfs, the same collation, the same verity and simplicity in his children's stories, the same passions, the same furies in all their speech. He saw that he was lacking a daughter-in-law, and, at the same time, that his two sons had done everything they had to do to in order that she should not be lacking. The King and Queen of the

Alzophages understood, just as clearly, that they had one too many sons-in-law.

Babillon, outraged by Aazul's imposture, wanted to confound him in the presence of all those who had the most interest in the clarification of the verity. She launched herself into the arbor with so much precipitation and fury that the king and queen fell off her shoulders. The fall was terrible; fortunately, they were not injured.

The princess did not even think of apologizing to them; she was too offended and too emotional to perceive it. They recommenced then a scene of explications and clarifications that clarified nothing and only put more obscurity and bitterness into minds. Everyone gave a very embarrassing air of verity to which they said because, in fact, everyone believed that they were telling the truth and had the intention of doing so

However, Aazul agreed that he had only found the princess in the palace, and already considerably grown, whereas Zaaf had the advantage of having taken her away from the black barbet when she was only a ten-inch princess, and had not quit her for a moment since. That testimony was confirmed by that of the princess, which had great weight. She also added to it the confession of the most tender passion she had for Zaaf alone; she no longer hid it, and declared loudly that he was her defender, her uniquely cherished husband, and that Aazul was a monster and an impostor.

Those who do not believe in fays and their enchantments would have been very embarrassed in such circumstances. Fortunately for Babillon and her lover, people believed in them in the two kingdoms, with the result that, after a little reflection, the two kings, assisted by the best heads in their Councils, thought very seriously that the unfortunate Aazul might have been the victim of the malignity of Fierotine. That conjecture led to others; the black barbet was suspected of having been something very different from a barbet. Scarcely had that doubt appeared than it changed into a certainty, when Zaaf and the princess testified that, when they had thought the barbet dead, it had suddenly disappeared before their eyed.

Once the end of the thread had been grasped, everything became clear and explicable; a fay capable of enveloping herself in a barbet skin in order to doom a young princess could certainly adopt the face of a beautiful princess in order to seduce a young prince; she could build palaces by the dozen for that; the dwarfs and the collations cost her nothing. The proof that it had happened thus was that the palaces had disappeared along with the fake princess. Thus, everything was explained, and everyone was satisfied, except Prince Aazul.

The two kings agreed that it was necessary to adhere to that idea and only try to discover, by means of some friendly fay, whether it was Fierotine or another who had deceived the prince.

That arrangement had nothing that satisfied Aazul; he was madly in love with Babillon; he persisted in believing that he was her husband, and sustaining it in spite of the respect he had for Kanor and for Alzopha. He could not hide his fury and went out menacing Zaaf and the princess with avenging himself for their perfidy—which is what he called the tender attachment that they had for one another.

Kanor hoped that reason and time would bring his sons back to milder sentiments; there was no longer any thought of anything but rendering thanks to the gods and informing the people of an event whose consequences would interest them so strongly.

Alzopha, who was already old and had no heirs to his Estates but his daughter, thought that he could not do better, by adopting is son-in-law, than associate him with the Empire. The ceremony of his adoption and his coronation was indicated for the following day. It was to commence with sacrifices to the gods, followed by a repast worthy of the magnificence of the Kings of Alzophagia, as well as the games and fêtes that were to company it. Kanor was charged with containing Aazul within the bounds of respect and duty, or sending him away for a while.

The fays were invited, and they all came. Fierotine dared to appear there, like all those who had rendered services to the two peoples and who had nothing for which to reproach themselves. People dissimulated and heaped her with civilities and caresses; everyone knew that she was the heroine of the wood and the palace that the prince had inhabited, with whom she had played the role of the princess so well; another fay, her intimate friend, to whom she had made the confidence, had rendered her the small service of betraying the secret at the earliest opportunity.

Kanor sent in search of Aazul, in vain; he did not appear, nor did a few words who were his friends. It was learned that they had departed for a hunt that was to last a week. When malcontents absent themselves on a day of celebration and pleasure, they are not missed; people only enjoy themselves all the more; their presence is a burden of which they are disencumbered.

The sacrifices and the ceremony of coronation took place with a great deal of pomp and tranquility. Alzopha wanted Zaaf to take his name, as he was going to reign over his subjects, but the Kanoris opposed it, and by a unanimous agreement of the two nations he took the name of Kanor, which was a presage that he would reign over the two peoples and unite them.

The feast even passed without sacrifices, with a great deal of order and gaiety; nothing was more curious than seeing Their Alzophage Majesties, six inches tall, with about thirty princes, lords and ladies of their court, sitting around a table with sixty place-settings, the other thirty of which were occupied by as many Kanoris nine or ten feet tall; all of them were mixed up, and arranged in such a fashion that there was a Kanori next to an Alzophage. The consequence was that from a certain distance, the table appeared to be only half full, and on drawing closer, one might have thought that one was seeing thirty giants, each of whom had an Angola or a marmoset beside him. But the Alzophages no longer sensed that humiliating disproportion; the hope of soon seeing it end seemed to make them grow in advance. The example of Babillon also gave all the ladies a courage beyond their strength.

After the meal, there was dancing until the end of the day. Aazul thought he could profit from that moment to abduct the princess, and, by the favor of the commencing obscurity, he and those accompanying him slipped into the hall where Babillon was. Whatever care he took to hide, Fierotine, who did not lose sight of the princess, was the first to see Aazul; apparently, she suspected his design and wanted to take advantage of it for a second time.

As she no longer had any power over the princess and could only take her form a second time by rendering her invisible with her consent, she approached Babillon and told her briefly what she thought of Aazul's design.

She admitted everything that had happened, in order to gain her confidence, promised to repair it in future by greater services, and, to begin with offered to deliver Babillon immediately from a lover who could only displease her and harm her a great deal, in the circumstances. Fierotine admitted to the princess that she was in love with Aazul; between women, those sorts of confidences win the heart at a stroke and bring about a solid reconciliation. The fay promised to take him so far away and keep him for so many years that when he came back he would no longer think about abducting anyone.

Babillon, who could not doubt Aazul's evil designs and feared their effect, not only for herself but for a prince who was much dearer to her than life, consented to everything. Fierotine gave her a ring that rendered her invisible by placing it on the little finger of the left hand, whereas, worn it on the little finger of the right hand it was simply an embellishment.

What a pity it is that those rings are not common! What a pleasure it would be always to have one on the right hand, except sometimes, at certain moments, when no one would neglect to put it on the left.

At the moment when the princess, furnished with the ring, disappeared from all eyes, the fay took her form; thus, the exchange could not be perceived by anyone. Under that disguise, which had already succeeded so well, Fierotine soon separated from those who surrounded her and approached Prince Aazul, who tried to hide. After having looked at him with an air of mystery and benevolence that he had not expected she left the hall and went out into the garden.

The opportunity seemed to the prince to be too good to miss; he followed her, along with all of his troop. Fierotine, pretending to perceive him and to attempt to flee, ran as fast as she could toward a gate where the prince had placed his horses and the rest of his men, so that he saw her take that route with the greatest pleasure.

No kidnapper was ever better duped by an abduction; he was the one who was abducted. When the fay reached the gate, where she was expected, and saw the ambush and the prince's horses, she uttered screams that she knew full well would not be heard, and did not omit any grimace that might complete inducing Aazul in error.

Delighted by the success of his enterprise, he took a route that led to the sea, where he had a boat that was to take him to a distant country. There he would lead the most delectable life with the princess, who would not fail to love him—such was his plan.

Believing that he was following that route, however, he took another; his arrangements were not those of the fay and she was the mistress of the carriages and the roads.

She had misled and dissipated all of the prince's retinue; he still thought that he was surrounded by his men, who were hobgoblins clad in their forms and loincloths. With a layer of mist an inch thick, which the fay placed between her and those following her, she deceived them, and separated them for as long as she thought necessary.

Aazul therefore, traveled all night, thinking that he was heading directly for his little ship; but when daylight appeared, he commenced to have a presentiment of his adventure on seeing, not the shore of the sea, but a dense forest. Soon, he no longer doubted the trap when he saw a palace. He would have liked not to enter it, but he

sensed that he was being conducted instead of conducting.

Scarcely was he there than the fay no longer con-
strained herself; she quit the face of Babillon and resumed her own, which had nothing that was not very
unpleasant. However, she declared to the prince, forth-
rightly, that she loved him and wanted to be loved by
him; she made a merit of having deceived him once before, under the form of Babillon, in that same palace, and
of having abducted him once again: all of that proved
her amour; but what use is it to prove one's amour when
one does not inspire it? The prince, who did not have
any obligation to her for her sentiments, did not feel disposed to any gratitude.

She made his see all the treasures of her palace; he
was not touched by them—but let us leave him to defend
himself against the enticements of the fay, to indulge in
petty cruelties, and finally to attract her indignation and
her vengeance; it is time to return to Alzopha's palace.

Everything there was in confusion and disorder as
soon as it was perceived that Babillon had disappeared.
A few little Alzophages, who were taking some fresh air
sitting under dwarf trees, had seen Fierotine pass by in
the form of the princess; they had recognized Aazul and
the men of his retinue running after the fake Babillon;
they carried the alarm into the hall. In a moment, nothing
was any longer heard but cries of despair and vengeance;
everyone ran to take up arms. Prince Kanor commenced
by wanting to kill himself people; prevented him from
doing so as best they could; eventually, no longer knowing anyone, he wanted to kill everyone.

Babillon was not sorry to see, in passing, how she
was loved, which made her prolong her incognito for a

few minutes. Finally dreading, however, no longer being able to contain so much fury, she passed her ring from the left to the right hand and reappeared, more beautiful than she had ever been. People scarcely recognized her; those who saw her were still in doubt, so much had anger troubled them.

Prince Kanor took possession of her, in a fashion to make it known that she would not escape him. Carrying her in his arms, he took her to the apartment destined for them. Thus that great day ended.

Babillon told her husband about the confidence of Fierotine, and showed him the ring. She told him that that Aazul had come with the design of abducting her; that Fierotine had preserved her from that misfortune by deceiving the prince again, as she had done in the wood, under a borrowed face; that he was in her power; and that, according to all appearances, he would not soon be delivered from the amour that the enchantress had conceived for him.

Whether Prince Kanor sometimes had need of that ring, whether he borrowed it, whether his wife wanted to confide it to him, or whether she often made use of it herself, history does not inform us. The day after, Aazul's adventure was common knowledge; he was regarded as lost, and people consoled themselves for it. The men who had accompanied him returned after a time, rather embarrassed and shamefaced.

In the end, more precise news was obtained from two Kanori lords whom the fay had separated from the troop and who had entered the magic palace with him. She had metamorphosed them both, in his presence, into little dwarfs, deformed and hideous, threatening him with the same torture if his indifference continued. Finally, weary and indignant at his refusals, she had treated him in the same fashion and had kept him in order to serve in her palace. It was thus that she used her former lovers, who were know as reformed lovers, as well as those whom she had not had the good fortune to please, and their torture only finished after a century or two. As for the two Kanoris from the prince's retinue, she had sent them back in order that they could convey the news to the two courts of Kanor and Alzopha.

From that moment on, Aazul was a drowned prince, and his brother united all suffrages. No one in the two kingdoms thought about anything any longer except pro-curing the fate of Babillon and Prince Kanor by the same means that they had employed, and which had succeeded for them—which is to say, by a mutual and sincere love. That made beautiful passions, fidelity and constancy fashionable.

The effect was certainly felt; the Alzophages grew visibly and the Kanoris shrank to the same extent. Soon, it was shameful for anyone to remain big or small: it was a sure proof that one was incapable of loving well, or that one had nothing capable of inspiring a true passion. That purged the land of fops and coquettes. When a little lord put on airs regarding his good fortune, people said to him: "You're the most amiable man in the world, but you're not growing; you only have a few inches." There was no reply to that; it was necessary to resume a mod-est tone.

Alzopha died of old age and Kanor of chagrin at the enchantment of his son. Prince Zaaf, under the name of Kanor, united the two realms and made a single nation out of the two peoples. He lived happily with his dear Babillon, whom he always loved as much as he was loved by her. She gave him a large number of princes as handsome as him, princesses as beautiful as her. He had the satisfaction of seeing, in a very short time, almost all the Alzophages grown, and treated by Amour as he had been himself.

The motto of the sovereign, and of his subjects, was: *True love works miracles*.

MINET-BLEU AND LOUVETTE

Intelligence without looks is very little, beauty without intelligence is even less. The fay Louvette, as everyone knows—everyone, that is who has some knowledge of the court of the fays—was, for five days a week, a very small person of frightful ugliness; for the other two days she had a majestic stature and a ravishing beauty. It is not to lose everything only to have two good days a week, when one can make the most of them, but one inconvenience rendered that advantage useless, which is that in changing face she changed her soul, character and sentiments.

On the five days of ugliness she was tender, good, gentle, passionate and as amiable as one can be with a repulsive exterior and a face that displeases. She employed those five days of ugliness in obliging people, flattering them and seeking to please; she spared no effort to find a genius, an enchanter or a mere mortal capable of attaching himself to what is called true and solid merit, that of the heart and the sentiments; she made attempts with regard to everyone, but nothing succeeded for her. However, if the good little fay made so many enticements and advances, it was not because she was a coquette—it is as well to be informed of that, because there was a slight resemblance—but because it was written that she would only recover her original form, which had been very attractive, when she had made herself loved veritably in her ugliness. That sentence was traced in the book of destiny, of which everyone knows the name although no one has ever read it.

One might suspect, however, how she had attracted that disgrace; it was by disdaining the sighs and scorning the prayers of a detestable, maleficent, ugly enchanter more powerful that her; those are events so ordinary that one has to need to spell them out, but if you do not state them there is always some blocked mind that cannot divine anything, and will charge you with a crime.

Louvette had, as has been said, two days of a ravishing beauty; she united in that short interval all the graces that can attract and please the eyes; if she had been mistress of conserving the same sentiments, which did not produce anything in her ugliness, she would have captivated and charmed the world; she would not have found a heart made to resist her. But in becoming beautiful she became stupid, proud, disdainful, and unbearable; her arrogance, her scorn, her lack of sentiment and taste—in brief, her attitude—drove away those that her face had attracted; it was sufficient to talk to her and listen to her immediately to lose that opinion and the natural desire to find a beautiful person accomplished. Beauty alone commences by placing it in the hearts of all men, but it needs something more to sustain it there, and in Louvette, everything concurred in banishing it therefrom.

She could not instruct either those who adored her when she was beautiful or those whom he would have like to persuade to love her when she was ugly that she was the same person in those two different forms; that was one of the conditions of her metamorphosis and the return to her original state. It was thought at court that there were two Louvettes, one beautiful and one ugly. It was at the court of the fays that all this happened; I don't know if I have said that, but, as it needs to be said, it is as well to say it here as elsewhere. The court is a country, in which people sometimes see everything and in which, also, they sometimes do not pay attention to anything, with the result that it was a long time before anyone noticed that the two Louvettes never appeared simultaneously.

Meanwhile the little fay had the chagrin, for five days a week, of being the joke and the reject of the same lovers who had, for the other two days, a disposition to adore her that she rendered futile by her manners, and by her lack of taste and return for them. The situation was rather sad, so Louvette was, indeed, very sad, and even more so on the days of beauty that those of ugliness—which proves that it is better to be ugly with intelligence and sentiments than to be beautiful while lacking everything else.

Such was her condition when destiny offered her a person as ill-treated as herself, and for the same reasons. He was a young prince; that is expectable; what is not expectable is that his name as Minet-bleu, which came not only from the singular blue color of his eyes, but also the garment of changing blue taffeta that he wore all summer long, and which he had first brought into fashion, suddenly taken up by all the agreeable men of the court, including the musicians and other talented individuals. He had originally been one of the Adonises over whom all the women agreed in going mad, without quite knowing why.

When those universals, those men of the day, appear, the old fays are not the last to run to them; they are so badly received by those messieurs that they certainly ought to correct them, but does one correct faults that one loves? The fay who experienced the rigors of the handsome Minet-bleu, punished him for it immediately; there are debts of honor for which an outraged fay never asks for an instant's credit. She treated him as the enchanter had treated Louvette; perhaps the two malevolent individuals knew one another; perhaps they had tipped one another the wink. The only difference was that Minet-bleu was only endowed with a repulsive ugliness, accompanied by all the merit of the heart and charms of the mind, for two days a week, and conserved for the other five his original beauty, deprived of everything that could make something of it: devoid of soul, intelligence, taste and sentiments, as indifferent and cold as a automaton, he only looked in order to see, and talked in order to talk, without ever giving the impression of thinking or feeling.

Minet-bleu's two days of ugliness and sensibility were precisely the same ones when Louvette was beautiful and indifferent; and the five days when she was ugly and sensitive were the same ones when the prince enjoyed all the charms of his cold and inanimate face. It was in the latter condition that he had to make himself loved in order to get out of it. He was even condemned to inspire a veritable passion in a woman of merit, in which he was even more maltreated than the fay, who could make herself loved in her ugliness, because it is more difficult to please when one is incapable of loving than when one does not have a lovable face.

The conformity of the two adventures of Louvette and Minet-bleu produced the effect that it naturally would produce. The prince, in his two days of ugliness, fell madly in love with Louvette, who was then in her two days of beauty; he was received with all the outrage and scorn of which she was capable; but once those two days were over, the prince exacted his revenge; poor

Louvette reentered her time of complete ugliness, while the handsome Minet-bleu recovered his ice and scorn with his lovely face. The fay wasted in her turn with regard to him the gazes and sighs that seemed to render her even uglier. That is the privilege of confirmed ugliness; everything harms and augments it, principally the very things that make beauty better.

However, the prince's court was soon deserted. The coquettes who had initially been amused by his pretty face and the prudes who had been dazzled by it, wearied of his impolite and excessively consistent coldness; only Louvette, who had no choice, remained attached to him.

Men are more incorrigible than women; their self-esteem is more blind and more tenacious; with the consequence that, although they made no more progress with the fay when she was beautiful than the women made with the prince in his beauty, they took longer to take it as read. Scarcely had two lovers retired, repelled by that insupportable beauty, than new ones appeared, ready to augur better of their talents and their merit. Because of that, Louvette, in her ugliness, enjoyed with regard to her lover an advantage and a pleasure that he did not have in her regard when she was in her beauty. That pleasure consisted of almost always being alone in the company of the one she loved, and not having a rival to witness the indifference of which she was the object; that was not a small consolation. Although that indifference did not diminish, at least it did not appear to increase; that was another consolation. Everything that nourishes hope is the wealth and the most genuine charm of amour.

Minet-bleu, on the other hand, was the butt of the insults and scorn of his beauty; in the presence of his rivals he was always the most maltreated. What torment!

Fortunately, he had so much intelligence that he took less harm from all that ill-treatment that another, but did he suffer any less for that?

That stormy court was often renewed; Minet-bleu was its doyen; no outrage had been able to repel or banish him. At first, no one paid any heed to that, but after a long time it was noticed, and gave rise to gibes. He held firm. His constancy seemed prodigious; women made a few reflections about it; they resolved in consequence to have pity on him and to try for that reason to forget his face, even if they had to give him audience with closed eyes. It was understood that he must be something extraordinary; the fashion set in, and in no time at all there was a woman of good appearance who made it a serious affair to steal that lover from "the insupportable beauty"—for Louvette, in her two days of beauty, was more commonly known by that name than any other.

History does to say whether the prince responded in the fashion that was hoped to all the generosity with which everyone wanted to heap him at once. Louvette, who found him detestable in his assiduities, found him even more so in his absences, and punished him equally for both; everything was good in order to torment him.

It is appropriate to remark in passing that, when once an ape becomes fashionable, he has the talent of sustaining it better than another; the taste that one acquires becomes a fury in no time.

A certain fay, known as Confidante, found that she was the only one at court who had not yet had a private conversation with Minet-bleu. Confidante was at least as beautiful as Louvette, but she was even more insensible, with the result that in favor of her recognized insensibility, the other fays forgave her for her beauty; although it was a bad quality for a confidante, they trusted her nevertheless; none had yet been trapped by it; she had the best heart and the best mind of any fay at the court. At the end of the day, she could not be reproached for more than two or three indiscretions and as many caprices. Characters as even-tempered as that are very rare, so hers enabled her to be generally liked by all her companions. She knew, therefore, everything that they knew regarding the merit of the ugly Minet-bleu; she knew so much that the curiosity that is the daughter and mother of all the woes that arrive down here, came to give her the bad advice to steal the prince from all his conquests.

Of all the tyrants that dabble in governing the head of a beauty, curiosity is the most absolute, although there are others more powerful; when it speaks, all the others shut up to listen and hasten to serve it. The fay Confidante had frequent opportunities to speak to Minet-bleu; she was charged in his regard with all the trivia and all the little secrets of her companions. As soon as she had made her decision, she made her charge—which is to say that she spoke on her own account and let it be divined that she wanted the prince to listen. He had acquired more experience in one month of good fortune than one acquires in ten years of study, with the consequence that he divined more than anyone wished, which is known as divining accurately.

Those who are on a level plane in what is called character might perhaps wonder how Confidante, being so insensible, could suddenly become so different, and so passionate for an ape. But have I said that she loved him? Not at all. She was curious, and nothing more. Curiosity resembles everything, but is nothing; it resembles love, hatred and all the passions; it can take on their appearance, just as it can quit it.

Confidante did not enjoy the confidence and error of her companions for long; they all agreed in detesting her and speaking ill of her. They joined forces in order to steal Minet-bleu from her, and that theft was no longer treated as an affair of taste but of honor, politics and vengeance. They applied themselves to it very seriously, therefore, and Confidante, whose curiosity might not have retained her with the little wretch for more than twenty-four hours, found herself engaged by pique, self-esteem, and the necessity of putting up a good defense.

Her enemies regarded the insupportable beauty, who was Louvette, as the person who ought to avenge them; the prince's passion for her was well-known; they therefore worked to inspire in that fay, not curiosity, nor amour for Minet-bleu, but aversion and jealousy for her rival.

Anyone who thinks that jealousy cannot be born without amour is badly mistaken. It can come from aversion for a rival, pride, self-esteem, or the desire for a preference that one does not want to employ, without being able to resolve to see another profiting from it. That was the species of jealousy that the fay stimulated in Louvette's heart. It did not take long for them to produce it; one woman alone can do the impossible in that genre working upon an another; it is easy to imagine what many fays working together can achieve.

Louvette, guided by their advice, soon hated her rival as perfectly as anyone could desire. She did not love Minet-bleu yet, but she had a keen appetite to render Confidante and him very miserable. She made a pleasure and a study out of doing both of them bloody turns and employing against them what are known as the ruses of war.

She interrupted all their conversations and rendezvous. Sometimes she affected airs of languor and passion, which gave birth to hopes in the heart of the prince; at other times she exerted herself to thwart the interest of her rival. At times when Minet-bleu could have been with Confidante, she occupied him; she appeared to want to listen to him, and to commence to love him; at times when she had no fear of that rival, or when Minet-bleu hoped for the recompense for the sacrifices she had demanded of him, she treated him with a despairing harshness.

At any rate, she saw him for longer; once the project of vengeance began, she was with him more often, and alone with him more often. I do not know whether anyone can divine what happened. This is it: that whole game of jealousy and vengeance produced on her the same effect that curiosity had produced on Confidante; in believing that she was only imitating jealousy and passion, she became all the more so because she had initially had a contrary design. It is thus that Amour plays with our projects; that is how all his games end up.

As soon as Louvette began to perceive her illness she began to take care to hide it—a futile effort, which only produces further betrayal. Fortunately, Minet-bleu loved her too much to perceive his good fortune as promptly as he would have done if he had not been loved as much. That change produced another: gradually, the prince's ugliness began to diminish.

That metamorphosis happened so slowly that it was almost imperceptible for the others, but it made great strides in the heart and eyes of Louvette. Every time she saw him, she found him more lovable, and that was exactly what he needed to become even more so.

The fays soon suspected that nascent amour; they had gradually avenged themselves on Confidante; they had counted on also avenging themselves on the prince, in view of what they knew of the character of Louvette—as if Amour does not make characters entirely anew when necessary!

The ugliness of the prince, which was already no longer ugliness, since it had to cease and cease by virtue of amour, was succeeded for five days, as you know, by Louvette's ugliness, which, until then, had appeared to increase rather than diminishing; but a fortunate hazard came to her aid.

The handsome Minet-bleu, parading his indifference and his charms in a nearby wood, was attacked by a gang of brigands. As can be imagined, he defended himself with a great deal of valor, wounded the most aggressive and dissipated the rest, but he came back with his left hand pierced by an arrow. The wound was slight, but the arrow was poisoned—which is of the utmost consequence, when one is not immortal. The surgeon who examined the wound said what he thought with all the discretion appropriate to such a case; however, he allowed it to be glimpsed that there was no other remedy than finding someone promptly whose mouth could draw the venom out of the wound by extracting blood. He added that there was a danger in that for whoever attempted it.

Scarcely had he finished speaking than Louvette, dissolving in tears, took possession of her lover's hand; she applied her lips to the wound, and whatever effort he made to withdraw his hand, she would not let go until she had drawn out all the poison by extracting all the blood with which it might be mingled.

The prince, more moved and more troubled by Louvette's action than by his injury and the danger he had been in, looked at her without having the strength to speak to her or to hold back his tears. Has there ever been ugliness in which there is soul, sentiment and veritable tenderness? No, of course not; so Louvette, in that state, appeared very beautiful to her lover—and was, in fact. When we perform a beautiful action, we do not have our ordinary appearance; we have the appearance and the features appropriate to the action.

Esteem, pity and gratitude entered at that moment into the soul of the prince, never to emerge again. He saw Louvette with entirely different eyes, and from that moment on she was no longer the same. A fortunate error is that which occasions a reality!

She lost her deformity and resumed her original charms, and as she recovered them, he became increasingly attached, with the result that in no time at all, she became the most beautiful of fays and he the most tender of princes. He also became the most handsome in his two critical days, as the insupportable beauty lost that name to become amiable and tender.

Things were taken on either part to such a degree of perfection that they recognized one another as being the same persons who had caused so many woes in their double form. Everyone else recognized them too, saying that they had suspected it, although no one had actually thought of it.

It was that point that destiny wanted them to reach before uniting them. As that was the only thing that remained to do, and both of them wanted it sincerely, no obstacle was raised to it. The Queen of the Fays performed the ceremony, and ordered fêtes that were among the most brilliant, according to connoisseurs. Louvette communicated immortality to her lover, in accordance with the privilege of faerie. He made very good use of it, and at the moment when I am writing this, they are still as happy as on the first day.

THE ENCHANTER'S MIRROR

To Madame la Marquise de Pompadour

Madame,

It is in vain that you would like to protect merit in secret, encourage the arts and talents, and procure aid and benefits for the virtues, without receiving any eulogies for it; quills fall silent but hearts speak. In refusing, Madame, eulogies and tributes that are truly merited, it afflicts those who owe them, and very little is gained therefrom; they maintain silence out of respect for your orders, but that very silence publishes what you wish to hide. Mine will be no more discreet; it will prove to you, I hope, all the respect with which I am, Madame,

Your very humble and very obedient servant,

Fagnan.

PART ONE

The enchanter Mirzaf spent his life sadly in an old castle constructed on a rocky escarpment on the edge of the sea. He only employed the secrets of his art in setting the surest traps for the birds and wild animals that he hunted in the forests near his retreat. He had never loved anyone, when he saw Princess Narbe, who was walking on the shore.

Narbe was the daughter of the King of Persia, and carried in her face the air of grandeur and majesty that announces and betrays sovereigns, even in slavery. She had come to offer her prayers in a temple of Neptune constructed of shingle at the entrance to a little wood beside the sea. Her heart was stirred by the emotion she had just experienced while imploring that terrible god; her eyes were still moist with tears that had just flowed for a cherished lover: for young Coroes, who was on the point of marrying her.

That prince was at sea; the most violent storm had separated one of the ships accompanying him, which had been wrecked two days ago on the coast of Gaza, without having been able to give news of the prince.

Narbe was walking alone, her women following her at a distance; her eyes were fixed on the sea, so calm at that moment, which was the end of a beautiful day, but she remembered fearfully the furies of that perfidious element; she was interrogating it tremulously regarding the fate of such a dear absentee.

Those dispositions gave the princess an air of distress and tender languor that rendered her extremely touching. Mirzaf was struck by that, as by the apparition of a divinity. He fell to his knees, addressed prayers to her as if to a goddess, and offered her his heart, his treasures, his secrets, his hand, and immortality if she were a mere mortal.

Mirzaf had a face that was scarcely agreeable; he caught her, in any case, at a bad moment. Coroes was a charming prince, he was beloved, absent and in danger; a woman in love is neither coquettish nor flirtatious in such circumstances; the heart is too occupied for anything to divide it. The enchanter was poorly received, repaid for his offerings with marks of the most offensive scorn. The princess continued walking without looking at him or responding. Motionless with anger and chagrin, he did not have the strength to follow her, and soon lost sight of her.

Coroes arrived the next day; the preparation for his marriage with the princess had been made a long time ago; the lovers were united. Narbe, all her prayers answered, remembered then those that had been offered to her on the sea shore; it was without anger and with a sort of pleasure. It is thus with almost all our ideas; those that have wounded us in a time of distress amuse us in a moment of satisfaction.

Mirzaf was only instructed of that news by the mockery of which he learned that he was the subject at the court of the newlyweds; although he was not wicked, he nevertheless resolved to avenge himself is a manner appropriate to poison all the pleasures that Narbe seemed to be able to promise herself.

Beautiful, young, in the highest rank, united by choice and by taste with the most amiable prince, and loved recklessly, such a happiness seemed to be above the reach of envy, but it foundered before a fatal mirror that the enchanter placed adroitly on Narbe's dressing-table. It was not that the mirror made her appear ugly in her own eyes; on the contrary, the glass was very accurate, and as the princess was very beautiful, she had never seen herself so advantageously, and with more pleasure, in any other; she would have been very happy if that had been all that she was able to see; but she also read the hearts and penetrated the most hidden sentiments of those she perceived there.

That redoubtable mirror only had the virtue of revealing the interior of anyone who was represented to it for the eyes of the princess; it was to pass from age to age, and from the dressing-table to dressing-table of all of Narbe's female posterity, destined to trouble the repose of the unfortunate princesses who possessed it successively. It could only break in the hands of a woman who saw in it, during the course of a year, her lover equally constant or her husband equally faithful. It is understandable that such a condition did not render the mirror fragile.

Along with all her court, Narbe was unaware of the effect of that dangerous present; however, it operated marvels. Every time the princess had occasion to perceive someone in the glass, whether they were present facing it or sideways, the person was revealed; the past, the present and a little of their future was shown to the princess; all his thoughts and the recesses of their heart were developed for her: a strange situation that leads to being content with almost no one, and discontented with everyone!

More perfect and a thousand times more lovable than anyone at her court, she was the least loved; one fears so naturally eyes that divine, but those that do more than divine, however beautiful they are, are found to be unsustainable.

Narbe attributed to notions and certain prejudices the knowledge and impressions that she obtained from her mirror, but people did not fail to complain of her penetration as an injustice and an excess of malignity.

Those of her women who were obliged by their estate to witness her at her dressing-table every day, and to appear assiduously before the mirror that denounced their most secret thoughts, experienced a continual torture; no matter how they composed their behavior, their faces and their expressions in one fashion, if their heart was otherwise inclined, Narbe unmasked them, and knew their secret thoughts better than they did. She enabled them to see that they had not deceived her, often by whispering to them what they wanted to say to her; she always said it generously, but that did not matter; it was saying it, developing what the most adroit dissimulation had hidden profoundly.

One expressed her attachment and respect in the most seductive terms, accompanied by the best calculated actions; it was so much wasted effort and preparation; her heart hid discontentment, impatience, annoyance and chagrin. Narbe saw all that, and broke down the dissimulation in all its retrenchments. Another had had a lover only the night before; another was only beginning to conceive the design of an infidelity; another, by means of sighs and glances, had permitted some hope: the princess was alerted to it by her mirror; she could have made a journal of it, and knew its slightest circumstances.

Meanwhile, hatred was redoubled in that excessively enlightened court; people regarded one another reciprocally as so many spies and Arguses who informed the princess. The lover most capable of keeping quiet passed for indiscreet and perfidious.

It was not in the most beautiful women in the court that Narbe perceived the most jealousy and enmity; it was in those who believed themselves wrongly to be beautiful, or who were chagrined by not being; it was from those that she received the most excessive and the most dishonest eulogies. One, with eyes apparently dazzled by the extreme beauty of the incomparable princess, with exaggerated compliments on all her charms, diminished them and criticized them in the depths of her heart, finding her forehead too smooth, her eyebrows too dark. Another praised her present complexion, while rejoicing secretly that it appeared less vivid and bright than it had the day before. Another advised placing a beauty spot beside some charm, or putting a flower or a diamond in some curl of the hair, because she thought to would have a bad effect.

*

Narbe sustained these vexations patiently for as long as Coroes was faithful to her; the term of a year marked by the enchanter had almost elapsed; a few more days of constancy and the mirror would have broken in the hands of that fickle husband; but Zama appeared in the court and the mirror was no longer in danger; Coroes became infidel; and what a rival Zama was! She had barely reached that dangerous age, the first flower of youth in which even ugliness is not without a few charms, and Zama possessed all charms in combination.

The varnish of freshness, innocence and gaiety that renders beauty so piquant embellished Zama's slightest features and actions. Such is a beautiful flower ready to bloom; one judges the beauties still hidden in its bosom by those that have hatched, and every instant adds to those that appear by uncovering new ones.

Zama was related to Narbe; blood sufficed to unite them, but something stronger can unite two perfectly beautiful women, which is beauty itself, when it is at the point of equality and perfection, which does not permit base envy or jealousies. Narbe was therefore the first, and perhaps the only, woman in her court capable of loving Zama. Soon she felt that she was sincerely loved by her. The mirror, which told her everything without her knowing that it was speaking to her, enabled her to see her relative as tender and as true as she was beautiful.

Narbe was not jealous of any of the tender and passionate homages that her dear Zama revealed; only the heart of Coroes interested her, and she believed that there was only admiration there. That prince hid carefully a more vivid sentiment of which he was still the master, and although he was unaware of the property of the mirror, he did not approach it; no hazard had yet exposed him to being see therein; he avoided occasions to encounter Zama in Narbe's presence, and often even avoided the princess's gaze at the moments when he might have been able to yield to the charm of seeing her.

Narbe took for withdrawal and indifference what was actually the commencement of an extreme passion; she made the mistake that one makes voluntarily when one has a good heart devoid of experience; one praises too much the object of one's amity or amour; one enables all its charms and merits to be known only too well.

Soon, Coroes' passion no longer had any limits; he sought out the princess everywhere and followed her everywhere, but she was too assiduous at Narbe's dressing-table for him not to end up dooming himself there. For a few days he was placed in such a fashion that, unable to be seen in the mirror, he was not accused by her; but the moment finally came.

The queen often took refuge in the cabinet where the mirror as placed; she spent entire hours there alone with Zama in order to avoid the crowd; she made the same mistake with her friend as she did with Coroes; she talked continually to the young princess about the intelligence, the grace and the charming face of a husband she loved too much, and by whom she believed herself to be loved as much. She compared him to the most brilliant and most lovable people in the court, and it was always to give him the advantage of the comparisons; she recalled all the pettiness and ridiculousness of the courtiers, in order to prove that Coroes was exempt from them.

Oh, let us refrain from praising to our friends the merit and charms of our lovers; let them refrain themselves from remarking too much to their friends on the beauty and grace of their mistresses. In the heart of a man there is an extreme tendency to love the friend of his lover; the same disposition is in the heart of the friend for her friend's lover; amity is always the dupe of amour, in the same way that intelligence always is of the heart.

One evening, when the two young princesses had forgotten themselves in that occupation for longer than usual, the impatient Coroes came to surprise them; they were in front of the mirror, where, without either one appearing distracted from what they were taking an extreme pleasure in saying to one another, both were enjoying separately the pleasure of seeing themselves. There is no pretty woman who does not know the natural and mechanical division that one makes of one's attention between the mirror that reflects her and the circle that amuses her; that is executed without appearing to be, without anything being lost thereby. She attends to everything, she responds to everything, but does not lose a word of what the mirror says to her.

That position prevented Coroes from being able to avoid their gaze; they both saw him in the mirror at the same time, but what a difference the sight of him produced in them!

Zama, already too prejudiced by what she had just heard to the advantage of the prince, was in one of those dangerous moments when a single glance bears disturbance into a sensitive soul that had just been stirred; as she raised her eyes to look at the prince, she perceived in his for the first time the respectful and tender something that penetrates us at a stroke and is embedded in the depths of our soul; Zama felt the subtle poison gliding through her veins; she lowered her eyes and blushed.

But what a frightful spectacle for Narbe suddenly to see the entire soul of the adored object, and to see it so different from what she had previously believed it to be: to see not only a passion in her husband's heart of which she had been unaware until that moment, but also, at that same moment, to see its excess and magnification; to see born in the heart of her best friend the fire that she seemed to have prepared there herself by means of her confidence and her eulogies—all woes at once!

Her eyes fixed on the mirror, her body motionless and her mind bewildered, that violent state was interrupted by the dolorous cries she uttered in looking at her friend. Then, no longer having the strength to sustain her dolor, she fainted.

That event extracted Zama from the disturbance into which the tender and passionate gaze of the prince had thrown her. She was no longer occupied by anything but the aid of which the queen was in need. Her faint lasted a long time, and when she was finally brought to her senses by means of cares and remedies, she seemed only to recover the light painfully. Her sadness, her obstinate silence, her frequent and dolorous sighs, alarmed Zama and Coroes sincerely; they both still loved Narbe. It is not at the moment when another passion is born in the heart, or an infidelity commences there, that the object that it is ready to forget and betray ceases to appear dear; one is only fully away of one's change long after one has changed.

As Narbe had been pregnant for a few months, the long faint was attributed to that, and the sort of languor and continual sadness by which it was followed to the situation she was on. The physicians employed their art in vain to render her a health that is not in the juice of herbs when the principle of our malady is in the secret bitterness of our heart. She languished, and hardly ever quit her bed throughout the time of her pregnancy.

Zama, truly touched by her friend's afflicting situation, spent entire days beside her bed. She only appeared to be occupied by the cares and duties that tender amity renders equally precious to the friend who acquits them and the friend who receives them; she often accompanied them with the most touching speeches and the most sincere tears, but those speeches and tears further augmented Coroes' passion for Zama, and Narbe was no longer deceived by them. There are no tears more dangerous than those that prove the sensibility and generosity of the heart of a beautiful woman; those shed in response to misfortune are a thousand times less touching.

It is a very dangerous situation for two hearts that are commencing to love one another to have to share cares, chagrins, vigils, and a common anxiety and interest; one loses oneself, one goes astray; people comes to know one another intimately, to adore one another without saying so, in sharing thus, in communicating one's fears and one's ideas—but is not everything dangerous to a weak and tender soul? Did not the very tomb in which the famous widow of Ephesus was buried become a precipice and a reef?[5]

It was in the midst of those dolors, more painful than those of childbirth, that Narbe brought into the world a princess who was named Theazir. It was hoped, for a few days, that the birth of the child might produce the recovery of the mother, but they soon knew that the malady was without remedy; nothing could cure her. She was seen to wither, to be extinguished, and to die, like a beautiful flower that neither the cool of the evening nor the morning dew can any longer reanimate, because a gnawing worm has cut the root.

In the final moments, Zama bathed in tears beside her expiring friend, entirely given to amity and regret, no longer experienced the secret and perfidious charm of amour that causes everything else to be forgotten. Even Coroes, troubled by seeing himself so close to ceasing to be a husband at the moment that he had become a father, avoided appearing before Narbe; he was equally fearful of her gaze and that of her friend. While fearing the excessively tender and fully merited reproaches that she read in Narbe's eyes, he could not encounter Zama's without becoming even more culpable; he therefore fled

---

[5] The macabre exemplary tale of the widow of Ephesus, originally narrated in the course of Petronius Arbiter's *Satyricon*, was recycled by Jean de La Fontaine as one of his *Fables*, thus becoming very familiar in France.

two objects equally likely to lacerate him: an adored lover and an expiring and betrayed wife.

Meanwhile, Zama did not quit her dear Narbe for an instant; she rendered her all the cares and duties of the most sincere and the most tender amity; convinced that some secret pain was the greater malady and the true poison that would soon deprive her of her friend, she implored her incessantly to tell her the subject of her distress; she hoped to soothe it by sharing it, far from believing that she was the innocent cause of it.

Narbe, finally moved and vanquished by her entreaties and her tears, was no longer the mistress of a secret that she had resolved to carry to the grave.

"Why do you want to tear out my heart, cruel and dear friend?" she said to her. "It's you, it's your presence here, and it's your dangerous charms, fatal to my happiness and my repose, that have reduced me to the state in which you see me; they have condemned me to the death that is approaching rapidly; I shall fly into its arms without regret. I loved, I was loved; my life depended on the heart of a fickle man; I have lost it; it is you who have stolen it from me; you're perhaps unaware of it. May you not soon experience the same attachment for him and the same inconstancy on his part; may I alone by the victim; you are both dear enough to me and to one another for me to make that wish. Adieu, Zama; let me die."

Every word that Narbe had pronounced had pierced the heart of the princess with a pain so intense that for a long time she was mute and motionless; only the abundance of her tears depicted the state of her soul. How culpable she found herself at that moment! How many evils without remedy she had produced! But how strong despair and generosity render a beautiful soul!

Zama suddenly emerged from the dejection into which she had plunged. "No," she cried, "no, you shall not die, unfortunate wife, without at least knowing your friend. You, Sun, who see us and illuminate us, receive the prayer of a virgin who is devoted to your worship; our oaths are inviolable and sacred; no authority on earth can free us from them; hear mine and receive them. I swear by your essence and your light, by that of all the stars to which you communicate it, I swear and I promise to unite myself with the holy virgins who are in your temple before you cease to illuminate our horizon this day. Die, then, now, O Narbe, if you want to die; Zama can no longer reproach herself for your death; you cannot carry that fatal idea to the grave; it cannot follow me into the refuge I have chosen; your fickle husband can no longer enjoy your death or my life. That is determined; adieu, I am running to where the religion of my oaths summons me."

"What have I just heard, O Heaven, and what have you done?" cried Narbe, dolorously. "Why did you not warn me about a design so useless for me and so cruel for you? I would have prevented the effect; you know that religion forbids interrupting a virgin who has sworn the oath that links her to the primal star; you have abused your situation and mine, you have engaged yourself forever; you have tried to immolate yourself, alone and entire, to my repose: what a sacrifice! How dolorous it is to feel that it is for me alone that you have made it, and that I shall not enjoy it. However, I cannot hide it from you, too dear friend, that I experience a kind of relief in thinking that nothing can prevent you from accomplishing a vow so cruel to yourself; I sense how it will avenge me on my infidel; it seems to me that I will quit this world with less regret in leaving him prey to his remorse, and separated from you forever."

Zama could not utter a word in response; she was so gripped, as if astonished, by the oath that she had just made; she embraced her friend for the last time, and immediately went to bury her charms, her amour and her grief in the refuge she had chosen. Doubtless she experienced strange penalties there; those whom despair determines thus without return are condemned to futile and intense regrets.

Narbe had the pleasure of telling Coroes that Zama was lost to him, that she had entered the fatal temple, from which the authority of the sovereign could no longer extract her: the fatal pleasure of afflicting, and piercing the heart of the person one loves. How unfortunate are those who are reduced to no longer knowing any sensual pleasure than the one thus procured!

Coroes, incapable of dissimulating his rage, made it so evident to Narbe, expressing himself in terms so harsh and offensive to her, that he advanced her final moments without perceiving it. She was bathed in tears; she expired, but the prince did not see either her condition or her dolor. He was only demanding Zama, only pronouncing her name, and still reproaching her angrily for not having informed him of her friend's design while he might have been able to prevent its effect, when he finally perceived that Narbe was no longer in a condition to hear him.

In vain and too late, he tried to help her; she died in his arms.

The kind of delirium that seized the prince at that moment caused people to fear for his life for several days; he had loved Narbe too tenderly not to be sensible to her loss; charms that cease to touch us sometimes recover all their empire when death comes to separate us from them forever.

Narbe had all the honor of the prince's sadness and regrets; they lasted as long as his life; whether they were really sincere or whether he was groaning internally for the loss of Zama, he never pronounced any other name than that of his wife, and he renounced any engagement. His tenderness and his cares appeared to be limited to raising his dear Theazir, the unique and precious pledge of a union that ought to have been happier.

Theazir was brought up with all the care that there is no need to describe because it is easy to imagine; the intemperance and excess of attention, care and caresses were lavished upon her that every often spoil a person whom less art and preparation might have formed better; she escaped all those dangers; she sustained the surplus of lessons, excessive praise and base flattery—in short, everything that harms the great from the cradle onwards.

I have forgotten to say that she was beautiful: a quality so essential that it is a sin against the rules of art to commence a portrait of a woman with any other; it seems that one can only be interested in other qualities when one knows what pertains to that one. In order, therefore, to extract promptly from anxiety those who might have any on that subject, it is as well to advise them that at the age of four years, Theazir was already more beautiful than her mother, Narbe.

That might perhaps seem incredible to those who remember the enchanting features of Narbe, but nothing is so true; and what is also worthy of remark is that the attractions of that four-year-old marvel were augmented from day to day, and, so to speak, from hour to hour, so considerably that she had scarcely reached her tenth year that they were already irresistible. Nothing was seen at her court but infidel lovers and jealous and desperate rivals; no man could see her without surrendering his arms to her; she did not give liberty the time to recognize itself, nor the heart the time to respire.

Everywhere she went she became the center of all gazes, adorations and homages. What was even more charming was that, without appearing to suspect it and letting nothing be heard, she neglected nothing at all that as necessary to extend and conserve that empire. In a person of an inferior order, such a precocious gift might perhaps be reckoned coquetry, but in a princess it is humanity, pure bounty and nothing more; furthermore, rank, age and innocence had nothing to do with it.

The beauty that pleases men too generally, whether it is extended by finesse or whether it is only owed to a charm produced naturally, because it is the cause of it, ought not to be expected to please women equally; one cannot enchain an entire sex with impunity without revolting at least half the other, and without always being hated by those that have the most pretentions.

Young Theazir knew all that at a very early stage, and made her arrangements in consequence; as she was very cheerful and a little malign, she took particular care always to appear more lovable and more loved in the eyes of those who appeared to want her to be less in both regards.

That fashion of avenging herself often caused terrible revolutions in the health of the jealous individuals who were its object: vapors, oppressions, migraines, asphyxiations and vertigoes—in a word, every sort of epidemic malady—that could only find relief in the hope that the beauty of the princess would not be of long duration; that in growing older she might deteriorate; and in other mollifications of the same sort.

As Theazir's petty malice did not prevent her from having an excellent heart, when she perceived that things were going too far, she was careful to distribute those sorts of topics to those who had need if them. She had some informed that she had shadows under her eyes, that they had lost half their gleam; she had others told that her complexion was darkening and hr skin less smooth; and others a few similar trivia in conformity with the genre of their malady—and the poor invalids recovered visibly. She even took the attention further with one of the most amiable women of the court, who had taken the matter so much to heart that she was at the extremity. Theazir had her told secretly that she had smallpox, and in that confidence the invalid came back to life.

Until then, Theazir's charms had only shone within a small circle and were only known to a small number of fortunate and privileged mortals who had either the right or permission to enter the palace where the daughters of the Kings of Persia were brought up until the age of fifteen. That building, separate from the sovereign's, was inaccessible to all those who were not attached to the princess by some responsibilities, and when she emerged for some ceremony or religious duty, which only happened rarely, she only appeared so scrupulously veiled that it was impossible to distinguish any feature. However, Theazir's beauty had already generated rumor; renown had announced it even in the most distant foreign courts.

As soon as she approached her fifteenth year, Coroes, charmed that the new star was soon to illuminate his palace, nevertheless conceived a few anxieties; an ordinary beauty is less embarrassing; ordinary fashions are sufficient ether to dispose of it or keep it; but marvels and prodigies demands other efforts. He feared making as many enemies of all the rivals whom it was necessary to sacrifice to one alone. He wanted to choose a son-in-law worthy to succeed him, and at the same time he was determined to prefer the happiness and choice of his daughter to the political views that normally decide the destiny of sovereigns. How could he extricate himself from so many embarrassments?

This is how: he made the wise decision not to seek the remedy for the misfortunes until they arrived, for fear of attracting worse ones by trying to prevent them,. In the meantime, he thought about procuring himself amusements and pleasures. He therefore proposed to attract to the court what there was of the most illustrious and most brilliant in neighboring realms. In order to succeed in that, he had it announced that on Theazir's birthday, the ceremony of her first entry to the Palace of the Kings of Persia would be celebrated by a tourney, in which the most distinguished princes and knights in the realm would enter the lists, with all those who wanted to present themselves, the victors in which would be crowned by the hand of the princess. Her beauty had already generated too much rumor not to attract all the brave and gallant men in the neighboring States. No one at court was occupied any longer with anything but the preparations for that great day.

The king wanted Theazir to appear with all the splendor appropriate to the heiress of a great empire. Her household, which had only consisted until then of a certain number of women and necessary officers, was composed of the most distinguished individuals in the realm, and also the most accomplished and most appropriate to render her retinue as brilliant as it was numerous.

On the first day of her fifteenth year, therefore, Theazir emerged from her juvenile palace, never to return; she was mounted on a chariot so brilliant that the Sun's could not have been more so; it was surrounded by her entire retinue, and the immense crowd of the people was almost carrying it, crying: "Gods, how beautiful she is!" They could not see her, for she was still veiled, but they thought they could see her, which is the same thing for the people.

The princess was awaited in a hall where all the peers of the nation and all the Orders of the State were assembled; the king was seated on his throne, at the foot of which she prostrated herself; then he held out his hand to her and lifted her up. After he had removed her veil and embraced her, he had her sit down under the same awning. All the peers came in their turn, in accordance with their rank, to prostrate themselves at the foot of the throne and render their homage.

After that ceremony, which was very beautiful, but so long that it was beginning to bore the princess—because the most beautiful things are boring when they go on too long—the king gave his hand to his daughter and passed with her, followed by his entire court, into the apartment that was destined or her; it was the one that had been Narbe's. The princess was put in possession of all the gems, pearls, diamonds and jewels that her mother hand employed, which composed the most immense and most complete treasure that any Oriental princess had ever possessed.

The famous dressing-table, of which the enchanted mirror was a part, had been prepared and equipped with all the care and apparatus that an item of furniture destined for such an essential and serious purpose requires:

an occupation that gives employment to so many people and consumes so agreeably a time that it is absolutely necessary for great princesses to employ in that way, especially if they are very beautiful.

The ceremony of the installation in the palace, the opening and the first session of that dressing-table, was conducted in the presence of all the ladies of the court; thy all waited in silence until Theazir had taken possession of that little domestic throne before approaching her and rendering their homage. She placed herself there with a dignity and grace that enchanted the spectators, but scarcely was she seated before the charming seducer that presents the sweetest mages to self-esteem and beauty and even deceives and consoles ugliness, and scarcely had she spent a few moments, paying tribute to the charms of seeing herself and the voluptuous emotion that an entirely natural self-confidence gives when it is well-founded, than, casting a glance at the circles behind her, and of which the mirror, in showing the faces, also allowed her to see all their thoughts and secrets, she uttered an exclamation and a burst of laughter so explosive that it set the tone for the whole assembly. Everyone, therefore, started laughing heartily, without knowing why. The king himself was not spared

Seriousness returned by degrees, however; but the princess continued to laugh, and those what were able to imagine that they might have something to do with her hilarity soon became even more serious. Those who had not thought to begin with that they might be the subject of the laughter began to fear it, not seeing any end to it. A few withdrew, very piqued; others followed them, all as discontented. Soon, the crowd was beginning to melt away, and the princes was still laughing, although no one else was laughing, with the exceptions of a few insipid laggards, the mimics of the court who always want to exhaust imitation.

As laughter added to the beauty of the princess, enabling the sight of teeth such as no one had ever seen, of the kind that, without hyperbole, efface the brilliance of pearls and the most beautiful and select water, among the courtiers who did not know her and were seeing her at that moment for the first time, the most indulgent thought that, as she was laughing advantageously, she was apparently fully conscious of that, and must often laugh without any other intention than obtaining all graces therefrom. Others thought, quite simply, that her intelligence did not respond to her face, which they imagined all the more readily because the circumstance is not without example.

The king, who penetrated those different sentiments, was anxious and chagrined thereby. He regarded what had just happened as greatly to his daughter's disadvantage, the first impression that one gives to belief ordinarily being the one that remains and which characterizes us. In addition, he regarded Theazir's excessive laughter far more as a malady than as an ordinary impulse of joy. He therefore required all those who surrounded her to withdraw.

The object about which the mirror had just spoken to Theazir no longer appearing before her, it ceased speaking and she ceased laughing. The severe expression that the king had adopted gave the princess a seriousness by which he was as astonished as he had been by the excess of her laughter.

"Princess," he said to her, "what has just happened in the presence of so many witnesses, on an occasion when you have appeared for the first time to the eyes of my entire court, worries me and mortifies me equally.

There is little dignity, and rarely sufficient dignity, in immoderate laughter, and when it has no subject, there is no excuse for it. It is regarded as a weakness of the mind or a poor disposition of the body; I doubt that my subjects can take away any other judgment, and it has nothing agreeable either for you or for me."

Theazir lowered her eyes and maintained silence; then, suddenly, she threw her arms around her father's neck and held him in her embrace for a long time. Such a tender impulse soon spread over Coroes's face all the tenderness with which his heart was full. Then Theazir, resuming her ordinary cheerfulness, said to him: "I beg you, Sire, not to believe that I am either ill or feeble-minded, but at the same time, permit me to laugh a little every time I see what I have seen."

"What have you seen, then?" cries Coroes, with a sort of chagrin. "For after all, you ought to have seen all that there is of the most distinguished in my realm assembled before you to render you duties and respects, which has nothing risible about it."

"Sire," continued Theazir, "I have seen abundant exterior respect, but I have seen far more hidden jealousies; there were not, I believe, four of your ladies who were not on the point of choking on it, and that's the truth. At the same time I saw in the hearts of almost all the men, whose manner was very respectful, depths of pride, self-esteem, conceit and indiscretion that were, I confess, very amusing."

"But you astonish me even more," said the king. "How did you learn, pray, at the age you are, to read in the heart like that, to divine the interior sentiments of those you are glimpsing for the first time? Don't you know that that that's the most consummate and hazardous study, and that the knowledge in question escapes the most profound meditations?"

"I don't know," said Theazir, "what profound meditations can produce, nor what escapes them; you can judge that I haven't made any. However, without thinking about it, and without wanting to, I penetrated the most hidden sentiments of all those surrounding me, not only with regard to me, but all their designs, intrigues and affairs—in brief, their most secret thoughts."

"This is becoming curious and interesting," said the king, "but won't you make me party to your discoveries?"

"I don't owe secrecy to anyone," said the princess. "In any case, Theazir will always adore in you her father and her sovereign; that sentiment does not admit reserve. But where shall I begin? For instance, the tall, rather thin woman who was to my left, in a green simarre, who has very beautiful eyes, suddenly took mine in aversion at first glance, and I saw that as clearly as I see you."

"Very well," said the king. "That's Zegris, perhaps the most equable woman in the court, the least infatuated with her face, to such a point...."

"Wait," Theazir interrupted. "I saw, however, that she had been very smitten with a tall man who has a beautiful face, who was very close to you; the backcloth of his jacket and tiara were crimson.

"Right," said the king. "That's Almasen, the Crown Treasurer; gossip has said the same as you, and may people have believed it, because it's sufficient for it to speak to convince the greater number."

"I don't know what gossip has published about either of them," said Theazir, "for no one has said a word to me about it. Zegris and Almasen are new and unknown to me, like all those about whom I can talk to you. I saw, therefore that the lady so little infatuated with her face has only broken with Almasen because he has dared to praise another's charms in her presence. I also saw that a very short and replete man placed opposite her has been occupied for a week in making her forget Almasen, and that he has succeeded, although he has no other merit in her eyes than that of praising her charms, always in the same tone, all day long."

"What you're saying is quite funny," said Cores. "You're depicting the stout Nader after nature, for it's true that he says everything in the same tone, that he only quits with the dusk someone whose hand he has taken, and that he's as little varied in speech as in manners. But you know more than gossip, which hasn't yet informed of us this union between him and Zegris. We'll see whether it echoes you; that would be singular. But continue, I beg you."

"Did you notice," said Theazir, "a young woman of medium height, very pale, with a slightly round face and an admirable mouth, covered in diamonds?"

"I know who you mean. That's Zunika; she's a charming woman by virtue of the mildness of her character; made to give jealousy, and incapable of acquiring any; she's adored by all those who know her. I don't know whether she pleases you, but I'm certain that you've enchanted her; I perceived that."

"I was going to tell you everything that I've just heard, Sire, so you would have seen that I divine accurately, if you had not anticipated me," said Theazir, with a smile that embarrassed Coroes slightly, because he had taken a liking to Zunika a few days ago, and that liking was still a mystery. However, he read in his daughter's eyes that she knew full well what he was trying to hide.

She soon extracted him from that embarrassment. "Oh, I was about to forget the original cause of my laughter, the thing that appeared to me to be the funniest thing in the world. It was a woman of a certain age who was in the embrasure of a window, from which she was amusing herself looking me over and criticizing me from head to toe; it was on her that my eyes paused first, and I couldn't hold back; that woman doesn't appear to have lost anything of her original beauty, although she's already at a age where it's necessary to be resolved to losing it; I even believe that she would have been an accomplished beauty if there is a real and touching beauty devoid of grace; for nothing is so regular and so neat as all her features, but they don't please because they lack the adornment that comes from the generosity of the heart and the beauty of the soul; that, in my opinion, is the source from which all veritable graces stem—those I mean, anyway. The woman had a black mantle embroidered with gold and gems, and her jet black hair was heightened by a large ruby and flame-colored feathers."

"Right," said the king. "I suspected it as soon as you opened our mouth; it's Keleskir you're talking about; a woman of abundant intelligence and great knowledge; but continue—I like to hear you."

"That woman of intelligence and knowledge," said Theazir, "doubtless has neither intelligence not amiable knowledge, for I saw that she has loved a large number of your courtiers; almost all of them have been with her; at first I wanted to count them, but it would never end; some have only reigned for a week, others for four days, a few for twenty-four hours; the longest reign has not lasted a month; all of them have quit her, exceeded and repelled; all of them hate her and she hates them, furiously. I distinguished in the crowd the man who has reigned since yesterday evening; it's a young man not yet twenty, who is already feeling the weight of her chain and thinking of shrugging off the yoke, and she is thinking about punishing him."

"But if you're not mingling in your details recent anecdotes," said the king, "I believe that yesterday evening, one of the women in the retreat from which you've emerged must have been occupied in informing you of all that you know. But I confess that you're astonishing me greatly. Tell me about this adolescent whom you believe to have been attached to Keleskir's chariot yesterday evening. I want to clarify that fact and figure out, if it's true, where you might have learned it."

"It's the man who gave her his hand, tremulously, when she went out."

"That's enough," said the king. "I remember him, and either I'm much mistaken or you've made an error. I'll know which in an hour."

"Well," said the princess, "you'll do justice to my penetration."

She continued for some time to talk about everything she had seen, and told him things so particular and so secret, about things of which he was so well informed and so convinced that he was alone in being so, that he could no longer stand it. He forgot up, exclaiming: "Oh, I'm lost now. Either you're inspired or I'm betrayed— but no, that isn't possible; it would be necessary for me to have revealed to you myself what I assure you I haven't said to you or to anyone else. There something supernatural, an enchantment, in all this—but swear to me that won't reveal to anyone else what you've just told me. It's important to the repose of all those you've unmasked so thoroughly that your penetration isn't known. No one would dare to appear before you any longer. If this sentiment that I can't define continues to enlighten you, it must only be for you and for me."

Theazir promised that, and Coroes went out, recommending an extreme adornment to her for the fête that her presence was to embellish. The princess obeyed that last order exactly; the rest of the day and all the following day were employed in her attire, without losing a minute. That brief time passed like lightning; twice as much would have passed without ennui. Gold, brocade, flowers and diamonds were placed, distributed with so much intelligence, and even good fortune, that the costume appeared to be an artistic masterpiece, and her person a marvel of nature.

An immense esplanade overlooked by one of the sides of the royal palace was the place chosen for the fête, which consisted principally of horse- and chariot-races. The side of the esplanade opposite to the palace, which was facing it, was ordered by a dense wood; that wood was cut be a single road, which was as broad as the castle, in order not to limit the view; its length, in a straight line, was a league, terminated by a lake of such extent that the eyes was lost there, as in a sea. The square was surrounded and closed by barriers, which enclosed the area where the assailants were to dispute strength and skill. All along the left hand side of the square that separated the castle from the wood, amphitheaters had been erected with seven steps, destined for the portion of the bourgeoisie and the people who could contribute to the decoration by their adornment.

In the opposite side to the right, there was a single amphitheater in the middle of the space between the castle and the wood, on which a number of musicians were placed, in proportion to the area and the distance over which they were to be heard. The remainder of that side was closed by two barriers, higher than those in the field, which formed two vast emplacements made to contain the various assailants, their equipages, their horses and their retinues until the time came for them to enter the lists. The emplacement between the wood and the orchestra was for those of the nation, the one between the orchestra and the palace for foreign competitors. The terrain that remained empty between the barriers and the field, like the one that remained on the opposite side between the amphitheaters and the barrier, was still very spacious, and was destined for the people.

Two pavilions or grandstands, each of which formed a semicircle, were erected at either side of the principal entrance to the palace, one for Coroes and the noblemen of the court, the other for Theazir, the princesses and ladies of the palace, and her retinue.

The king and his daughter took their places, to the sound of the acclamations of an innumerable people, a noise more flattering and sweeter than the sound of the most melodious instruments. As soon as the cheers had died down, a herald gave the signal, he trumpets sounded, and sixteen horsemen entered the field. On the side of the palace that was the quadrille of foreign competitors; sixteen others appeared on the side of the wood; they were the Persians.

The prize that was being contested was that for horse racing; at all times the Persians have prided themselves on excelling in that exercise; the horse was always an animal of singular veneration among them, with the result that they took everything relating to it beyond anything that might be said, either for choice or for care, and for the art of handling them and making use of them.

The ones that appeared at that moment, either on the side of the lords of Persia or that of the foreign princes who had come to dispute the prize, were indisputably the most brilliant and best made that it is possible to see. The richness of the equipment—bits, bridles and so on—can be taken for granted, the sole adornment of a fine horse is the rider mounted on it; when both respond perfectly to what is expected, no one has eyes for all the rest.

That interesting spectacle commenced with a solemn march made by the two troops, which passed in turn before the stands where the king and the princess were, after which each quadrille performed maneuvers for its own part, in which it was impossible to match the charm, the ardor, the pride and the finesse of the horses, and also the grace and skill of those governing them; the spirited and impatient animals scarcely appeared to be touching the ground; meanwhile, the hands guiding them had such mastery of their movements that they appeared to be performing an accurate and light dance, every step of which was regulated and measured.

From the first moment, Zerica on the Persian side and Prince Enzalek on the opposite side attracted all eyes and shred all prayers. Zerica was a prince of the same family as Coroes; he was the bravest and best made of all the Persians and incontrovertibly the best horseman in the realm; he was mounted on a Thessalian horse that he alone had been able to tame; its long bristling mane, its glittering eyes and its foam-covered bit announced its impatience.

Enzalek was the eldest son of the King of Hyrcania, a neighbor and ally of Coroes. The successor designated by the choice of the entire empire, he was a mild prince with a noble and interesting face; he was riding the most vigorous and lightest horse that had ever come out of the mountains of Korea.

The race was the full length of the avenue to the edge of the lake that terminated it; an equestrian statue was holding a standard, that the person who was the first to lay a hand on it was to bring back.

Each quadrille was arranged in a line, one to the right and the other to the left of the two corners on the wood that formed the commencement of the avenue. Shortly thereafter the barrier was opened and the signal was given.

The two troops departed with a moment that was swift to begin with, but every moment saw it increase; soon, the rapidity of arrows would have been less prompt; already, they were half way along the career; no advantage was discernible yet, but in the blink of a eye, Enzalek and Zerica had drawn far ahead of the rest of the field and the victory only seemed uncertain any longer between those two rivals. A precipitating torrent and winds that pursue one another and collide would have been less impetuous in their course. As they approached the finish they were almost touching; there was not yet any advantage sufficiently marked to decide between them.

The advantage however, was on Prince Zerica's side; he was about to profit from it; his victorious arm was already raised to seize the standard; he was almost touching it, when, a gust of wind having agitated it, Zerica's horse was alarmed, reared up and leapt ten paces to the side, in such a fashion that all of the prince's skill was futile. He was witness to the good fortune of Enzalek, who took possession tranquilly of the signal of the victory.

The two quadrilles, mingled and confused, returned to the field, with the victor at their head. They traversed it to the sound of acclamations and instruments sounding the victory. Enzalek advanced toward the stand where the princess was, in order to receive the crown and the prize from her hand, and to hear and respond to all the pretty things that never fail to be said on either side in such circumstances.

But it was the custom and one of the laws of that court that, after the victory of one of the quadrilles over the other, the victor could be challenged by a single competitor from his party, so that if the victory had been to the Persian side, a Persian could have challenged the victor. In truth, the victor was master of refusing the challenge, but if he accepted it and he won a second victory, the prize was doubled and the glory incomparably greater; whereas the assailant was dishonored and passed for a vain and reckless individual if he were victorious—which rendered challenges rather rare. It was also necessary that the one who proposed it should not have been among those who had taken part in the first race.

I do not know whether anyone expected to see such a reckless individual enter the lists, or whether his arrival gave pleasure or pain, but I know that the trumpet rendered the shrill sounds that announced that a new competitor was approaching.

He appeared, entered the field and came straight to Enzalek. He saluted him and raised his hand toward the standard that the prince was holding; that was the signal of the challenge.

The stranger appeared to be no more than twenty years old; he had the air of a hero, without losing anything of the tender air that a lover ought to have; he had the face of Mars and that of Amour, mingled and fused into one. He eclipsed everything that had shone before his arrival; on seeing him, one ceased to see everything that had been remarked before he appeared. An involuntary movement attracted all hearts and fixed all eyes upon him alone. No one knew him but everyone respected him, and more than that; everyone loved him.

After having contemplated him for a few moments with a sort of proud and jealous admiration, Enzalek seemed to be suddenly drawn by an impulse of affection; he embraced him tenderly and handed him the standard, which was the sign that he accepted the challenge.

Enzalek's action pleased the king and the court extremely, as well as the princess and all the people. At first there had been a great silence at the arrival of the stranger, as if everyone feared that he would only encounter a refusal on the part of the victorious prince, and everyone was equally satisfied that Enzalek had accepted the challenge with a good grace; applause and cries of joy rang out in all direction.

The two rivals approached the stands where the king and the princess were, in order to as their permission to begin a new race; it was granted to them, while offering eulogies to the generosity of Enzalek and the boldness of the newcomer.

The standard was immediately handed to a herald, who went to replace it, and the two princes went to the barrier from which they were to depart—for it is as well to remark that the stranger ceded nothing to Enzalek with regard to the nobility of his blood; his name was Estereza, which is all that can be said of him for the present; there will be an opportunity to know more about him in due course.

Thirty of Enzalek's slaves were holding by hand as many horses, in order that he could choose one for the second race; the one for which he settled appeared to be even finer than the one that had just been victorious; it was an impetuous Arab that he could barely contain. Estereza was mounted on a jet black horse, all of whose movements were so lithe and supple that it appeared to be gliding over the arena rather than walking; its equipment was covered with diamonds and pearls of great value, which announced both the wealth and affection of its rider.

The trumpets gave the signal and the barrier opened. Enzalek departed like lightning, while Estereza hardly seemed to be moving; the advantage that the Prince of Hyrcania gained at the beginning of the race seemed so considerable, and he conserved it for such a long time, that no one was any longer doubting his victory when, suddenly and rapidly, Estereza was seen to draw closer to his rival, reach him and overtake him, as if by enchantment—for Enzalek's efforts and the speed of his progress could be distinguished by the movement of his horse and his own, whereas Estereza and his charger seemed motionless, moving so rapidly that the eye could scarcely follow them. In the same way, soaring hawks or eagles pierce the clouds to swoop down, cleaving the air and traversing immense distances without appearing to move their extended wings.

Estereza reached the target, took the standard, rejoined his rival and tried to hand the sign of victory back to him, but Enzalek refused it, with the same generosity that he had shown before. They returned to the field together, without it being possible to distinguish by their manner which of the two had won the race, so modest did the victor appear, and the loser so scantly consternated by his defeat.

Another singularity was that Enzalek still had a part of the agitation produced by such a violent movement, and his horse was covered in foam, whereas Prince Estereza's horse was as cool as it had been at the moment of departure, and he was as tranquil himself. He soon lost that tranquility, however, as he went past the stand where Theazir was; a disturbance, the precursor of grand passion, took possession of his soul: the useful and dangerous disturbance that announces and anticipates us in the heart of the object that causes it.

The princess felt all its force; she saw and heard the prince without either seeing him or hearing him. She circled his head with a crown, and made him a present of a tiara enriched with valuable diamonds, without daring, or being able, to say a single word. He received those gifts in the same fashion, with the result that the state in which their hearts found themselves at that first moment did not permit them to give or to receive more—at least, they both believed so.

Nothing, however, is better given or received than what is given and received in that manner; that silence and those faults, which communicate a shock that no one else perceives at first, is worth more for us and for the object who causes and shares it than all the seasoning with which indifference and the freedom of the will enable us to accompany our actions.

In his turn, Enzalek received presents from the hand of the princess proportionate to his rank and his merit. She also made considerable ones to the foreign princes and Persian lords who had distinguished themselves, and all those gifts were accompanied by graces of which the princess knew very well how to make use; delicate and measured eulogies were distributed with all the art and finesse of which she was capable.

The embarrassing stranger whose presence had nonplussed her no longer embarrassed her; she was free and returned to herself; he had passed on to Coroes's stand, where he received the praise given to his merit modestly. The eyes and ears of Theazir had followed him there; she did not lose sight of him, but at least she saw him at a comfortable distance.

It seems that there is a pain in seeing too soon and at to close a range an object that is beginning to please; it has the same effect on the heart as an excessively bright and sudden light has on the eyes, in oppressing and dazzling them. However, that pain is undoubtedly voluptuous, since the memory of it is always dear. That memory already occupied the princess entirely.

The competitors who were to dispute the prize for the chariot-race had left the field. Estereza, who was numbered among them, had gone with them. Theazir could no longer see him; she was occupied with her idea. She said to his image everything she believed that she ought to have said to him at the moment when her hand had crowned him. She reproached herself for her embarrassment and her silence; would he not have thought that she lacked politeness or intelligence? But he had appeared just as embarrassed himself; what was the cause of his disturbance? What was his name, his country, his rank, his birth? Was he worthy of the sentiments he inspired and capable of responding to them? How many uncertainties and torments at the same time!

But he reappeared, and the dreads, the doubts and the sad ideas vanished from the heart of the princess; the sight of her beloved is the dawn of the most beautiful day for a woman in love; it dissipated the darkness and expels the clouds. But what! Can two people be lovers for having glimpsed one another for an instant, without speaking to one another, without knowing one another?

Yes, undoubtedly! Seeing one another, hearing one another and knowing one another develops and justifies the amour that ought to be born of a first glance; it does not augment it.

But let us see the chariots, and those conducting them.

As in the first race, there were two quadrilles, one composed of Parisian lords, the other of foreign princes and noblemen. Each quadrille of four chariots hitched to six horses abreast. All the chariots were admirably constructed; gold, ivory and varnish were employed therein, with all the precision and elegance that distinguishes our modern artists. The teams of horses responded to the magnificence of the vehicles; the harnesses and the reins were all brilliant, well-designed and chosen, polished to such an extent that the eyes were dazzled by them.

Those chariots were guided by noblemen whose good looks and skill were above all expression. The most distinguished among the Persians was Prince Zerica once again, and in the foreigners' quadrille it was Prince Enzalek, but the unknown victor, the young and charming Estereza, effaced them all.

His chariot did not resemble the others either in its form or its adornment. It was a kind of marine monster, the large head of which, bristling with scales and a crest, formed the front; the back and the tail, curved back in a semicircle, formed the depth and the rear of the vehicle. The chisel of a skilled sculptor had imitated the fins and scales of a monster perfectly; the painter had grasped the nuances and the tone, and the excellent varnish that covered the changing green-brown that was the background color of the dragon gave it a gleaming sheen like that produced in scales by the water and foam of the sea. The whole was rendered to such a degree of perfection and verity that the eye was alarmed by it.

The chariot was harnessed to six horses of a dazzling whiteness, of an incomparable mold and finesse; nothing was as simple and simultaneously as rich, as their adornment; its consisted of supple tethers and cords whose fabric was pure gold, without any mixture of other colors; the studs of their bits were diamonds mounted in rose settings, almost as large as the ones that our bourgeois woman wear in the ears when they are rich. Those roses, however do not adorn them as well as they adorned Estereza's horses.

He was standing on the chariot, with one leg advanced and extended over the neck on the monster, as if he had just slain it; his superb head was ornamented by the crown with which Theazir's hand had embellished it; for there are no ornaments that embellish more than those of victory, when they are placed on the head by the hands of Amour. The son of the nymph Clymene emerged less brilliant from his father's palace when he confided his chariot to him in order to illuminate the world.[6]

All gazes presaged victory for him; all the hearts that he had won desired it. Theazir's went further; it said no prayers for an eventuality of which it already had no doubt; her conqueror appeared to her to be invincible.

The trumpets gave the signal and the barriers were opened; all of them gave their horses free rein at the same time, and an equal movement carried the eight

_____

[6] The Oceanid nymph Clymene is credited with numerous sons by several different myths, but the one cited here is Phaethon, fathered by Helios.

chariots away, in the same way that a fresh and light wind impels ships quitting port and makes them disappear, flying, fleeing and seeming to decrease, becoming lost in the open sea.

The same ardor, the same skill and the same desire to win held all the rivals in the same line for a few moments, but soon, the chariots of Enzalek, Tamor—and Arab prince of extraordinary skill and strength—and Estereza obtained a marked advantage over the others.

Those three rivals began to approach the end of the course, and that decisive moment required new efforts and skill; the victory did not consist merely of arriving first at the end of the career; it was also necessary to take a scimitar placed in the middle of a circle of stones, disposed in such a fashion that unless one approached them very narrowly it was impossible to reach the sword; if they were approached too closely, the danger of breaking up against them was inevitable. The scimitar, the symbol of victory, was upright, at hand height; it was a matter of seizing it precisely enough to be able to draw it from its scabbard without slowing down.

Scarcely had the impatient Tamor seen the diamond-enriched hilt of the scimitar glinting in the distance than, pressing his horses, which had only too much ardor, they carried him away in such a fashion that he could no longer govern them, nor retain them. He employed his strength and skill in vain; no longer sensing his hand or knowing his voice, his chargers broke his chariot against the boundary-stones; the broken axle shattered into shards and the prince was thrown to the ground, which doubtless prevented him from being dragged for a long way by his own horses.

The violent impact and the debris of Tamor's chariot, with which the ground was covered, became obstacles and a reef for Enzalek; he was only able to approach the boundary-markers by circling around them, in order to pass close to them on the way back; it was no longer possible for him to change hands and pass from the left to the right, because Estereza had directed his course to pass to the right of the stones at the same time as Tamor or Enzalek passed them to the left; he was the master of the right, and closed the passage at the moment when Tamor's chariot broke up on the other side. The unfortunate Enzalek seemed only to have arrived so close to the goal in order to get a better view of Tamor's fall and Estereza's triumph; the latter's burning wheels skimmed the boundary-stones so closely that the redoubtable steel of the scimitar was shining in his hand before anyone had seen him render himself master of it, so rapid had his course and his measured action been. It is thus that the bird that announces spring seizes its prey on the surface of the water without wetting its wingtips.

Only seven chariots returned to the field, because of the accident that had happened to Prince Tamor. Estereza was at the head, even more redoubtable and charming than when he had departed; he appeared so to all eyes; one can imagine that those of the princess judged him even more advantageously.

He approached her stand in a manner as respectful as the first time, but more gallant. His respect was less timid; there was something nobler and more definite about it; that was held to his credit, for that is the advantage of pleasing: everything is good, everything succeeds. Timidity is a sentimental tenderness; the contrary is nobility of the soul, the consequence of his birth and good education; even faults take a fortunate turn in the mind when the heart is seduced.

Theazir had the pleasure of crowning the prince a second time and handing him the rich presents that were the prize of victory. He expressed his gratitude in terms most enchanting for the princess, and she replied in a fashion most appropriate to augment the value of her gifts.

The other princes and noblemen who had competed in the race also received marks of the princess's generosity, but although she accompanied them with eulogies as flattering as those she had lavished on the prince, employing either the same terms or others that could pass for synonymous, the expression of the sentiment was not the same—and how much expression adds to words!

Thus the great day finished. Estereza had the honor of giving his hand to the princess and conducting her as far as the apartment of Coroes, which she entered alone with the sovereign, that place being inaccessible when the king was there with his family.

A superb meal was served in one of the halls of the palace for the foreign princes and the Persian lords who made up the quadrilles of the two races; they were to eat in public and to be served by all the ladies of the court and Theazir's household.

Prince Zerica, who was the nearest relative of Coroes, was charged with doing the honors. As the victor in the two races, Estereza was the one to whom they were due. Coroes and his daughter had reserved the pleasure of witnessing the fashion in which that fête passed; they placed themselves for that on a platform overlooking the hall, which was closed to any gaze, by means of which they could see without being seen.

A few precautions had been taken only to allow entry to the hall to as many people as it could contain without impeding the order of the service; the competition was prodigious. The table was admirably well decorated and served; the circle that surrounded it formed an enchanting sight; it was composed of the forty noblemen of the two races, all of distinguished rank, with interesting faces and of accomplished merit. Each of them was served by three ladies.

In order to avoid the embarrassment of preferences, care had been taken not to give either the ladies the choice of cavaliers, nor the latter the choice of ladies. Lots had decided that, but it seemed that fate took pleasure in making just distinctions in conformity with tastes. All the ladies merited, by appearance and rank, being served by those to whom they were presently rendering services; they acquitted it competitively with so much dignity and grace, and their services were received in such a respectful and gallant manner, that they seemed to be commanding queens, and the cavaliers they serves as many slaves taking orders. The obliging distractions, decisive preferences, marks of eagerness, mute and expressed jealousies—in sum, the enchanting trivia—occasioned by the service, as piquant as they were futile, were innumerable.

The three ladies whom the lot had assigned to Prince Estereza were, incontrovertibly, the most charming in the court. They were beauties of the first order, who could only be compared with one another; they had the same advantage over the other ladies that Estereza had, incontestably over the other cavaliers, with the result that nothing was better matched. If Venus had ordered her three Graces to serve Amour, she could not have set a more agreeable scene before the eyes, so that charming tableau attracted the principal attention, in spite all the charms spread throughout the entire circle and the ensemble.

As you will not have doubted, no other object shared Theazir's attention; she envied the fate and the employment of the three beauties who surrounded the prince; she looked at them in turn with an anxious jealousy. However, Estereza conducted himself in a manner to reassure her; he was polite and respectful with his redoubtable ministers, but he was serious and distracted.

Can one ask any more of a lover surrounded by and besieged by three beautiful women than distraction? The more he has, the more he obliges us. But the prince soon lost that obliging distraction, by virtue of a hazard that seemed very cruel to the princess.

Among the ladies that were serving him there was one who prevailed over the other two to the same extent that they were above all the rest. That was young Kemiskir. She was of illustrious birth and even more worthy of the highest fortune by her sentiments than by her birth. It was impossible to see anything more beautiful and more touching than her face when it was animated. Many people preferred her then even to Theazir, but that charming spectacle was the rarest thing in the world; proud and seemingly cold, to the point of insensibility, no passion decorated the superficial varnish of those beautiful features, without which they only spoke to the eyes, and said nothing to the soul. Her complexion had the whiteness of lilies, but it also had their uniformity; it was an admirable whiteness but always of the same tone, devoid, except in rare moments, of the hint of pink that rendered it so beautiful.

Kemiskir, formed like a nymph, a head taller than her two comparisons, was serving Estereza with all her beauty, pallor, seeming coldness and pride; she was to his right, holding a vase full of an exquisite wine, with which she was preparing to fill a golden cup that the prince was holding. Doubtless, in spite of her cold appearance, she was only too sensible; her gaze was fixed on him; she neglected to turn it away at the moment when she was about to pour the wine into the cup. Estereza had a similar distraction at the same moment, with the consequence that the wine was poured over the hand and garment of the prince, without the person receiving it or the one pouring it perceiving the fact.

Scarcely had Kemiskir perceived the effect of her distraction than disturbance, shame, chagrin and amour appeared in her face in all the colors that were never seen there, and which suited her so well. In that condition she appeared so new, so different from herself, that a general cry of admiration went up. The prince also blushed; from that moment on, his eyes always sought Kemiskir's; they often encountered them, and the most vivid colors no longer quit her throughout the evening.

Theazir did not miss a single one of their movements; for as long as the meal lasted she experienced all the dolors that a nascent amour engenders when it believes itself to be unfortunate.

She was finally delivered from that torment; the feast ended and the foreign princes were conducted to the apartments in the palace destined for them.

As soon as Estereza was alone and free to interrogate his heart regarding the impression it had received, he found it divided between two opposed sentiments, each strong enough to tear it successively.

The Persian princess had initially excited the most vivid admiration and emotion in him, so adorable had she appeared to him. All his reflections still justified that initial judgment, but how beautiful Kemiskir, forgetting herself and losing herself in the charm of seeing him, had appeared to him! How that single moment had assured him that he was loved, and how many charms that certainty had!

He spent all the time in which he was able to avoid slumber in those agitations, loving alternately the two most beautiful women that were then in the world—and, in consequence, loving neither one of them sufficiently.

The next day, however, he went to the king's *lever*, along with all the peers of the realm and all the foreign lords that had been at the previous evening's feast. He appeared there in the noblest and simplest attire; a few diamonds comprised all his adornment, but they were of such great value that it was easy to see that they could only belong to a sovereign. One of those diamonds attached to his shoulder a crimson mantle; another sealed the cluster of white feather with which his coiffure was covered, and only three made the attachments of his jacket, which was a uniform green cloth.

That rich simplicity was imposing; although he was unknown in the court and even Coroes did not appear to know him, the king treated him with a distinction and preference that set the tone for everyone else, because they never escape sovereigns unless they do not know where they place them. In fact, Coroes knew full well that the prince was one of the sons of Maadi, the King of Palmyra, his friend and ally, for whom he had always had a singular esteem. Thus, the most illustrious blood flowed in the veins of that young Arab; he counted among his ancestors the famous Zenobia;[7] he had her soul and all her features.

Coroes knew that the prince in question was little known even in his father's court, and not at all in foreign courts, because he had been brought up in camp, and since the age of ten had not quit the armies that the King of Palmyra had been obliged to maintain at the extremities of his realm to resist powerful enemies against whom he had to sustain continual wars.

Estereza had been taken out of the army by the King of Palmyra and sent to dispute the prizes of the races; he had no other instructions than to conceal his name and his birth; he believed himself, therefore, to be quite unknown to Coroes, as he was to all his court; he did not know that the two sovereigns had discussed his marriage with Theazir, that they were in accord, and that everything was settled, in the event that Estereza pleased the princess; that was the sole condition on which Coroes had made the secret engagements he had contracted depend, wanting Theazir's choice to be free and that she might begin by giving her heart to the man who would be the master of her hand and the Empire.

The more Coroes studied and became acquainted with the young prince, the more he was charmed by his appearance, his sentiments and his intelligence; he wanted his daughter ardently to see him with the same eyes. He could not recall certain things he had noticed the previous day, during the races and in the stand veiled with gauze, without hoping that his daughter was already prejudiced by the same sentiments. He promised himself

---

[7] Zenobia was the queen of the Palmyrene Empire from 260-267 A.D., and Queen Mother until 272, when her attempt to conquer large parts of the Roman Empire ended in defeat.

to study her at every opportunity furnished by that second day, the pleasures of which were a kind of dramatic performance and a ball.

After a few moments of conversation, of which the only topic was the pleasures of the previous day and their magnificence, the fashion in which a number of the lords present had distinguished themselves—principally Estereza, on whom, following their sovereign's example, all the courtiers lavished praises—Coroes shut himself away with his ministers and charged the noblemen of his court to conduct Estereza and the other foreigners to Theazir's dressing-room.

She was receiving the ultimate advice of her faithful mirror on the most important points of her coiffure when she saw the brilliant squadron enter whose members had come to render homage to her. She was in one of those states of mind that render a beautiful woman so touching, in seeking carefully everything that might add to her charms, because she had been overtaken by horror on seeing those of another triumph over Estereza's heart.

She had been talking about Kemiskir with a few of her favorites; her distraction and embarrassment of the previous evening, especially all that coloring, so vivid and so rare in her, and which, for that very reason signified so many things, had been turned to ridicule in all possible fashions, but the princess was too interested in the cause that had produced those effects to participate in the pleasantries. The very absence of the young woman, who was said to be feeling unwell, further augmented the anxieties of the princess; she deduced therefrom that the prince had made a deep impression on her rival.

Those ideas had given the princess an air of dejection and mild languor that rendered her more redoubtable and more beautiful than she had ever been, so the sentiments of tender and passionate admiration that she inspired appeared in all eyes; but she only wanted to read what was in Estereza's. She saw them there with transport, and that sweet emotion of the soul, which is communicated so suddenly, and which immediately establishes the most intimate intelligence, rendered the prince so touching and so eloquent, and made everything that he wanted to say and everything that he said appear so tender that the princess no longer doubted her happiness.

When her heart had given itself for a long time to that dear object, the flower of her attention and her gaze, she remembered that it was necessary to represent indifference; she saw and talked to everyone; she responded to all the praise that was addressed to her with all the joviality and finesse that were natural to her; then she cast her eyes at the mirror again and saw Estereza therein for the first time.

Until that moment she had not had the opportunity or the time to address indiscreet glances to him. Scarcely had she fixed her attention upon him in the mirror for an instant than she knew that he was the Prince of Palmyra; that all the arrangements had been made between the two kings, that Coroes was only waiting before declaring the day of the ceremony for the opportunity to assure himself of his daughters veritable sentiments, and finally, that Estereza was not aware himself of such charming secrets.

So many agreeable ideas, which she regarded as presentiments, and which took on for her all the ascendancy of a verity that she could not doubt, without knowing to what to attribute the inspiration, gave her the same disturbance and the same blush that had disconcerted Kemiskir the previous evening.

That emotion had the same effect on the princess; it embellished her further, and lasted as long as the prince was present. She scarcely dared raise her eyes to look at him; however, she knew with an infinite gratitude that he was the son of a sovereign, which, very fortunately, dispensed her from blushing in secret and the sentiments she had had for him when he had only been a bold adventurer, which would have made her blush deeply if they had been misplaced. She was also glad to know that he was destined for her quite naturally, by the arrangements and political views of two kings.

Although the same mirror that had revealed those things to her also said something about Kemiskir and the impression that she had made on the prince, Theazir had not heard it, or made a semblance of not having heard it. She was in love; what a situation in which to receive advice! Our eyes see; our mind is convinced, but our heart is not, and it alone draws us forward.

The presence of Coroes, who arrived, did not contribute to diminishing the princess's embarrassment; he perceived that, and took pleasure in augmenting it further by whispering to her that he divined its cause. As soon as he was alone with her he said that he knew, and could not doubt, that Estereza adored her; he added, without giving her time to respond: "Confess, Theazir, that your heart has already told you what I am repeating to you; it has already spoken to you about the gratitude the Estereza's sentiments deserve."

Theazir tried to defend herself, but she did so in the fashion most appropriate to convince the king that he was not mistaken. He talked to her about the birth and merit of the young prince in the terms most appropriate to give her a high idea of him, and all though it could add nothing to the one she had conceived before knowing him, her joy and her questions were sufficient to betray her; and what completed dooming her even more fully was the vivid color that she could not hide when Coroes, in order to force her to agree to a verity that he already no longer doubted, said to her that the young prince was engaged to the most beautiful princess in the world, that he was to marry her in three days, and that he was leaving the next day to set the seal on that engagement.

A mortal pallor covered Theazir's face; her beautiful eyes closed to hide her tears; only a bleak silence expressed her dolor. But Coroes, who had caused it deliberately, soon put a end to it by telling her that she was the beautiful princess destined for and engaged to the son of the King of Palmyra, since he had been fortunate enough to please her; that all the arrangements had been made in secret between him and the King of Palmyra, but only on the condition that they were ratified by her choice. It was necessary then to confess that her heart ratified it, without complaisance playing any part in it.

She made that confession with good grace, and Coroes, after embracing hr tenderly, quit her, informing her that his intention was to unite her with the prince in three days, but that he did not want to declare it until the moment of the ceremony, in order to avoid the discontentments and objections that might be provoked by Estereza's rivals, who were powerful and numerous, and also to surprise all his subjects agreeably, who, without knowing the young stranger, had interested themselves in him to the point of wanting him to be worthy of their princess by birth, as they judged him to be by merit. The first reason was sufficient for Theazir to promise secrecy.

At the same time, Coroes had the Prince of Palmyra informed that he begged him to render to his apartment immediately by way of an indirect and secret path, which the person charged with conducting him would show him. Estereza went there with a sort of anxiety as to what might have led the King of Persia to give such an air of haste and mystery to the visit he was demanding of him.

As soon as they were alone, Coroes held out his hand to him and saluted him as the son of a sovereign who was his best friend and his ally; and, in order not to enlighten him partially, he set before his eyes his father's letters and the articles of the treaty made between them. Then he said to him:

"Prince, I wanted to know the dispositions of my daughter before informing me if yours. If hers had been contrary, I would have burned what you have just seen; you would not have known about your father's projects and mine; the secret would have died with us and you would have departed from my court without knowing that you had been known to me, nor why you had been made to come. What depended at first on Theazir now depends on you; we shall tear up these treaties if her person and her hand...."

"Oh, Sire, don't finish," cried the prince, embracing Coroes's knees. "The person of Theazir is utterly divine, you know that! Her hand could make the happiness of the greatest princes on earth. Give my heart the time to respire and to dare to believe that for which it had conceived every desire, but not the hope."

That transport pleased the monarch, although it was to be expected; it is a true present to a younger son of a good family to give him a princess of excellent beauty whose dowry is a crown. There was, therefore no more question of doubting or deliberating upon Estereza's liking; it was simply decided that the ceremony would be held in three days, and that the prince would keep the secret until then.

Independently of the equipage and retinue that he had with him, his father had made immense preparations and had sent an entire cortege, necessary to enable the prince appear in splendor; all of it was only half a day away, awaiting the orders of Coroes and the King of Palmyra's minister, who was secretly present at the Persian court.

These matters having been settled, the king announced that the fête to be held the following day, the third day of Theazir's anniversary, which consisted of various hunts, would not take place, but would be replaced by a fête of a very different sort, which would be held three days hence in his palace, for which he would make all the expenditure and preparations. He requested all those who were invited to it to appear there in the most brilliant fashion.

That change, and that mysterious announcement, was the subject of all imaginable speculations during the three days; everyone wanted to divine it and no one succeeded; curiosity and anxiety increased as the term approached, because no preparations could be seen inside the palace. The reason for that was that they were all made, and it would not require more than an hour to dispose and put in place everything that had been ready for a long time.

The second day concluded with the announced amusements, which were a theatrical performance and a ball.

It is not easy to define the form that the spectacle had; it had something of them all but did not belong veritably to any; there was music, declamation, singing and tirades, some calculated to draw tears and others to generate laughter, which often did neither in spite of their purpose. Nothing was as serious and as cold as the comedy of that people; their tragedy, by contrast, was often humorously ridiculous. They liked it thus, so much force does national prejudice have, and so easily is poor taste established. The seriousness of their comedy they called sentiment and mores; the gigantic exaggeration and ridicule of their tragedy they named vigor and sublimity. However, they were excusable, because they did not know yet the great rules that have determined taste, which have only been established since.

Let is return to the spectacle; it amused, or made a semblance of amusing, everyone—which is to say that it produced the same effect as most of ours; those whom it amused the least were not the last to decide for or against. Theazir and the Prince of Palmyra were extremely satisfied by it, because it procured them the means of talking to one another continually with their eyes, and even saying a few brief words, which were very clear in the circumstances they were in, although they were obscure to all those surrounding them.

The ball was no less advantageous to them than the play had been; Theazir did the honors thereof with an intelligence and grace beyond all expression. For his part, Estereza distinguished himself there; he shone with such a marked superiority in all the genres of charm and talent that are the soul of that pleasure that he pleased all the women without displeasing the men, which is the most difficult thing in the world, especially at a ball.

The day having terminated thus, no one was any longer occupied by anything but the expectation of the mysterious fête deferred by the sovereign for three days. That time went by too slowly for the impatience of some; it went too quickly for the immense preparations that a few others were meditating without knowing for what their attire would be employed.

The ignorance of that purpose threw a number of ladies into such an embarrassment that their heads were turned completely. They made representations and entreaties; they activated every mechanism in order to be enlightened as to what was planned; they would have excited and uprising or a sedition if they thought they could succeed by that means; no subject of complaint against the government had ever seemed more just to them. What, in fact, were they to choose? How can one make up one's mind, either with regard to color or coordination, when one does not know the usage that one is to make of a costume. Are there not conventions for every pleasure, and even fortunate and advantageous caprices in the fashion of applying oneself? Whatever taste one has, it is impossible to avoid clashes and ridicule when one does not know the connections that one ought to put into one's attire and the fête or pleasure for which one is dressing. Are there not nuances of gaiety or gravity in all of that, which garments ought to match appropriately? Was it necessary, therefore, that something that ought to be studied and planned with the greatest attentively should depend on hazard?

"It's enough to drive one to despair," said some. "We can't be held responsible," said others. "It'll be the death of me; no I can't appear under these conditions." In spite of the solidity of those arguments, and the bitterness of the plaints, with which the court and the city resounded during the three days, the secret was kept, and it was necessary to accept the risk of a clash of colors and accessories.

Theazir and her lover were not exposed to that danger; they were only too well informed of the subject of the fête. Independently of the hours when the princess opened her apartment, she saw Estereza secretly every day in the presence of Coroes; and those moments, so sweet, and further seasoned by the charm of an innocent mystery, had avoided for both of them the ennui of waiting.

Finally, the moment arrived.

The entire court was assembled in a vast hall where the royal throne was. The monarch appeared and took his place there. Theazir was to his right and Prince Estereza to his left; a primary singularity, which struck all eyes are the same time, was that the prince had quit the foreign costume in which he had appeared thus far and was dressed like the princes of Persia; his tiara even bore the mark of its sovereigns. In addition, nothing could be seen above the brilliance and richness of his adornment; Theazir's was no less striking.

Coroes did not leave his subjects in uncertainty for long. He informed them that Estereza was the son of the King of Palmyra; that his merit and his personal qualities, even more than his birth, had determined him to adopt him as a son and son-in-law by uniting him with Theazir. At the same time, he presented the hand of the princess to the fortunate Estereza, who received in the midst of cries of joy and the acclamations of everyone present.

While the king spoke to the peers of the nation, trumpets and heralds announced the same thing to the people, who had gathered in a large crowd in the main square of the palace, with the consequence that the marriage of Theazir with the Prince of Palmyra was published and spread everywhere at the same time. When it was firmly determined that the fête was a marriage, those who had dressed for a hunt or in some other idea, found themselves caught in the trap they had wanted to avoid, and begged the gods and humans to be witnesses to their innocence.

"Everything is ready for the ceremony," said Coroes. "Let us go to complete it in the Temple of the Sun, where the priests are waiting for us."

With that, he traversed the crowd of courtiers; giving his hand to his daughter, who had Estereza on her other side. All three of them took their places in a chariot, which seemed to be designed for bringing deities down from Olympus rather than for carrying mortals on earth, so rich and gallant was its structure. The cortege, the retinue and the livery all responded to it; everything was resplendent with gold and precious stones.

They arrived at the foot of the altars, traversing an innumerable crowd of submissive, loyal people who were blessing their master's choice, and only formulating prayers for the happiness of two such charming and perfect spouses.

Who would not have believed those spouses fortunate? How was it possible to imagine that anyone could be more so? Fatality of human destiny! How little it takes to poison the greatest benefits, to trouble the most perfect delights, and how ever-ready that small, sufficient dose of poison is, in the vicinity of the cup from which one flatters oneself that one will quaff pure, unalloyed sensual pleasure!

It was no longer a lover intoxicated by his happiness who was leading to the altar a pure bride, enchanted by his conquest; it was a distracted and pensive prince, who was giving his hand to an anxious and jealous princess.

What event, then, had caused such a prompt revolution in their hearts? Is it necessary to ask? It was almost nothing, but one of those nothings that almost never fails to become something.

It will be remembered that, since the moment when Kemiskir had been indisposed, or pretended to be, she had not appeared; but whether she really had recovered sufficiently, or curiosity had prevailed over her indisposition, she went to the sovereign's palace for the fête. Although she was no better informed of the subject than anyone else, her attire was so well matched to it, so noble and so gallant, that one might have believed that she had divined what it was. Alas, how far she was from thinking of it!

Estereza was the first person she encountered when she entered the palace; she was at the foot of the staircase that led to the princess's apartment; he offered her his hand. It was not without an extreme emotion that she saw the prince, and she was not in sufficient control of herself to hide it, and allow a part of it to be known.

Doubtless he imagined, in order to acquit himself, that he ought at least to say obliging things to her, but his imagination, heated by the idea of the moment that he was approaching, rendered him very tender. Instead of being, or only wanting to be, obliging, his face and his expressions had something so vivid, so touching and so true that when they arrived at the princess's apartment, Kemiskir was very emotional; and the prince appeared likewise.

The charming young woman did not have quite the same coloration that her face had acquired when she had poured the wine alongside the cup, but she had a part of it; in brief, she had enough to be extremely beautiful, and too much for a convalescent who had never been in complete health: too much not to displease Theazir.

That princess found it singular that, after four days of absence, the first thing that had offered itself to Kemiskir's gaze was Estereza; that it was by him that she was brought and conducted to her apartment; it seemed that there had to be design in that encounter.

The prince did not perceive anything at all that might wound Theazir; he did not even make, with regard to the anxieties that she had just conceived, any of the movements, either of repentance or tenderness, that might have reassured her. On the contrary, as soon as he had conducted Kemiskir to the apartment, he hastened to leave; he was awaited in the king's apartment, where he was to quit the Arab costume that he was still wearing in order to put on the Persian one with which he was to appear in the hall. The time was approaching; there was not a moment to lose.

His precipitation had no other cause than that, but it was interpreted differently; Kemiskir was suspected of having a part in it. The mirror then came to finish giving evidence against her; it confirmed very precipitately, in Theazir's mind, what the emotion and coloration of her rival had already said only too clearly; she knew, and was unable to doubt, that another woman adored the prince whose wife she was about to become.

The prompt and singular vengeance that she was shortly to enjoy prevented her from being wounded, to a certain degree; In fact, the unfortunate Kemiskir was about to learn momentarily that she loved a prince destined to bear another chain; she was about to witness the engagement and the good fortune of another. There is something delectable for a rival in such a blow, ready to depart.

Theazir, therefore, heaped Kemiskir with caresses, talked to her a great deal about the pleasure she felt in seeing her so fully recovered, in order to embellish the fête with her presence; she praised her charms, her attire, and her beautiful colors; never had she said such obliging things. She was only extracted from that malign occupation when someone came to tell her that she was waited by Coroes in his apartment; she went there alone, and everyone who was then in hers went to take their places in the hall.

Kemiskir was there, in consequence, quite close to the throne on which, soon afterwards, she saw Coroes sit down with Estereza and Theazir at his sides.

Every word that the sovereign pronounced was a thunderbolt for Kemiskir. She remembered, all at the same time, her rival's caresses and the perfidious sweetness of the prince before the fatal moment; she inferred that they had both known her sentiments, and that, in concert, they had wanted to insult her dolor, which she had only placed before their eyes in order to serve as their plaything and augment their triumph.

She could not sustain the impact of so many cruel and offensive ideas; she fell in a faint closely resembling death in its pallor and its chill; people attempted the usual help in vain, and it was necessary to carry her through the crowd in the condition of a dead or dying person.

The prince had his eyes upon her at the moment when she fainted, and by virtue of a natural reaction, he showed chagrin and alarm. Theazir's gaze, which was divided at that moment between her lover and her rival, remarked the full effect of the blow that Kemiskir had received and the full impression that her condition had made on the prince.

No one doubted that the beautiful convalescent's faint was a consequence of her original indisposition. People felt sorry for her; they criticized her for exposing herself to risk, for being in too much of a hurry to reappear, at the expense of her health. Only the princess thought differently; she did not search for the cause of the situation of a dying rival elsewhere than in the sentiments that she knew she had for the prince.

He too, remembering the tender and brilliant expression that seemed to have overtaken that beautiful face in two singular moments, each of which was marked by something personal to him, found that faint worrying, not daring to believe, and not being able to reject the idea, that perhaps he was the cause of the sudden malaise by which Kemiskir had just been attacked. He was moved and afflicted by that suspicion. One of our conceited fops would have commenced by making it a certainty and would have been amused by it, but more than four thousand years ago,[8] princes already had a better heart and better mind that those messieurs have today.

It was, therefore, in those dispositions, each of them agitated by different thoughts, that Theazir and Prince Estereza entered the Temple of the Sun. The torches and

---

[8] This remark, along with the subsequent reference to the scene being set "eighteen or twenty centuries" before the invention of gunpowder, is chronologically inconsistent with the earlier reference to Estereza being a descendant of Zenobia, but it does create space for the thirty generations that have still to elapse in the course of the story.

fire symbolic of their marriage were lit; they were united with all the ceremony and pomp imaginable and returned to the palace in the same order in which they had left it.

They were received there, and paid all the tributes that grandeur demands—which is to say that they endured all the prepared compliments, the speeches learned by heart, the oaths and homages of all the Orders of the State. In fact, it lacked nothing of what composes a celebration of that importance: numerous tables served with the most elegant profusion; admirable concerts in which the best music, executed with great precision, had no complaint to make of the words, nor the words of the music—which has never happened since—and games of every species; coffers opened at discretion for the convenience of ruined gamblers. It is even believed that there were illuminations and fireworks, although that is not certain, because gunpowder was not invented until eighteen or twenty centuries afterwards.

In any case, nothing was lacking in the charms of the fête, nor to the satisfaction of Coroes and the joy of his people. The sovereign, convinced that he had united two hearts formed to be one another's felicity, was even more sensible to the sentiment that a good father experiences than those that political views inspire in a sovereign who is assured of a successor capable of replacing him worthily.

Estereza appeared to love the princess tenderly; and, in fact, he did love her, and gave her proofs of it made to convince her of the fact, if she had not been wounded by the attention she had remarked in her lover for the condition of Kemiskir. How little it requires to trouble the repose and to engender the woe of a tender soul!

We left the beautiful Kemiskir in a rather parlous state. Scarcely had Estereza and Theazir returned to the palace after leaving the Temple of the Sun than they were told that she was dangerously ill. People did not fail to occupy themselves with her, as one does with individual misfortunes in the midst of public rejoicing— which is to say that no one any longer thought about her for a minute except the Prince and Princess of Persia. Both of them paid a particular attention to her, the prince by virtue of a sort of pity and a secret interest that he could not define, and the princess by virtue of a anxiety that stemmed from that very interest, which she had defined only too well.

Meanwhile, that beautiful person was soon at such an extreme point that, for a long time, people despaired of her life; but remedies, seconded by youth, sometimes work miracles. The danger passed, and it was only decided that the invalid would take a long time to recover, her illness originating, in the opinion of the physicians, from a sudden seizure and a violent chagrin, the cause of which was unknown and the consequence of which would be a melancholy and a languor that time alone could dissipate.

Without the aid of medicine, Theazir could discern the cause of the seizure and the melancholy clearly. Estereza sometimes believed that he knew it too, and while waiting until he could clarify the matter, he interested himself in the recovery of the invalid with a certain vivacity, which did not make Theazir want it very ardently.

Six entire months passed before Kemiskir was in a state to reappear at court. Although she had had time to accustom herself to the idea of seeing Estereza as the husband of another, she was in no hurry to show herself there, and was even more fearful of the frailty of her heart than that of her health; but a return was indispensable, and it was necessary to take that overwhelming step.

Kemiskir came, therefore to render her duties to the princess. She was still so depressed and so changed that, in favor of what she had lost of charms, she was almost forgiven those she had had before.

Estereza, who was present, scarcely appeared to pay any attention to her, or to recognize her. She did not remain for long in the apartment of the princess; her condition was a legitimate excuse, and thereafter, she was careful only to show herself rarely enough for the prince to notice the fact. However, as her health recovered, she recovered a part of what had rendered her so redoubtable in Theazir's eyes. The latter was not the only one to perceive it; everyone congratulated her for it. It would have been difficult for the prince not to do so as well; soon, his self-esteem was interested, and sharply piqued by Kemiskir's behavior.

He perceived that she never appeared to flee him, nor to seek him out. Apparently, he had counted a little in secret on that flight or that research, which came to the same thing. He remembered the vivid colors with which Kemiskir's features had been embellished twice in his presence, and those enchanting colors no longer appeared. Had he, then, been mistaken when he had thought that he had all the honor of the? That was humiliating; a movement of pride and curiosity engaged him to seek every opportunity to see her and speak to her.

He was far from believing that the sentiment in question was amour, or that it could become amour; however, it is thus that curiosity and pride are punished and metamorphosed in the company of a beautiful woman.

Theazir saw a part of those steps and divined the rest. It was him, in such good faith, who only hid them imperfectly; he was sure of loving the princess with all his heart; he had even been tempted, more than once, to tell her what he thought about Kemiskir's malady, and what he wanted to do in order to clarify the matter, so little finesse did he intend.

For her part, the languishing beauty, counting on having made her decision, became sufficiently mistress of herself to listen to the prince as often as he wished without any danger. She even found a sort of pleasure and a vengeance in not avoiding any occasion in which she could put on a show of her insensibility and her indifference. Alas, what scoundrel is more skillful in deceiving us than our own heart?

The prince soon became tender and pressing, every time he had the opportunity to be heard, entirely out of simple pride and pure curiosity—so he believed; and for her part, Kemiskir only listened by reason of vengeance; a least, she thought so. But she did listen; everything that is possible in that regard, it is necessary to expect to happen, because, sooner or later, it happens, unless one flees it very sincerely and very properly; for everyone flees, or tries to flee, but often one tries to too late; one only commences to want it when there is no longer time, and that kind of flight never succeeds. Kemiskir's pride, her designs to avenge herself and to punish the prince served her well enough at first; they gave her all the external appearances of indifference, coldness and even scorn; but what use are external appearances that our heart does not admit? It seizes a moment to betray them.

Estereza fell into a languor and dejection himself, by which his health was affected; he could not resolve to attribute it either to resentment or the chagrin of being deceived regarding Kemiskir's original sentiments; in fact, what did the present sentiments of that insensible individual matter to him. In what way would they have been wounding if she had not commenced by having contrary ones, and if she had not allowed him to see them clearly enough to count on them?

When such an error makes one ill, it is nothing other than pure passion, no matter what name it adopts as a disguise. For two months the prince was in that agitation without appearing in public and without quitting his apartment.

Kemiskir spent those two months without seeing him, and without perceiving that she was suffering from that absence, which she had not expected. She did not sustain it without a sort of anxiety, but ought not every good subject to have that naturally for a prince dear to the State? Besides which, one can want, to a certain degree, to be avenged on a lover who has not been able to divine how dear he is to us, but one rarely has a heart malevolent enough to want him to lose his life in consequence.

Such were the pretexts of which Kemiskir made use in order to justify to herself the agitation to which the absence and illness of Estereza gave rise. Finally, she saw him again, but it was with a trouble for which she was not prepared. He appeared so dejected, and had changed to an excessive extent that she had not expected; his languor had something so touching that she forgot, not only not to appear compassionate, but also not to flee after having appeared.

In vain she tried thereafter to recover the attitude of indifference that had hidden a part of her sentiments for some time from the person who had given birth to them; her soul showed itself entirely in her eyes, and the prince could no longer be deceived on that score—with the result that he soon loved recklessly, out of gratitude, the woman by whom he only though he wanted to make himself loved out of curiosity and pride. For her part, she repaid him by the most tender return of sentiments that had only appeared appropriate, to begin with to serve her chagrin and her vengeance.

Before the first year of her marriage had elapsed, Theazir had occasion to see in her mirror, more than once, that the knot that unified those two hearts had formed; she even found a consolation in that, and a vengeance of a singular species, in that she saw that Kemiskir, as faithful to her duties as to her passion, too proud to be the mistress of a prince whose wife she thought herself worthy of being, would not take the risk of repenting having loved too much if he became inconstant; and that, for that reason, the prince did not cease to be unhappy in loving an object so tender and so cruel as Kemiskir always was.

This, the fate of the fatal glass for itself assured for a second time; it would only break in the hands of a princess who had captivated the heart of her husband during the immense interval of an entire year, and Theazir was not in that situation. She therefore made the decision to give a number of princes and princesses to the State and to reign even more by her charms than her rank over all the hearts of her Empire, except for the heart of Estereza, of which his amour had made a sovereign exception. What a dolorous exception!

In any case, her situation was not the saddest; Estereza loved without any hope, and without any liberty, but that of loving. Few men are capable of that; they regard that state as the romance and chimera of sentiment; they all hope and pretend, more or less, even when they protest that they are loving without pretentions and without hope.

Kemiskir loved too, without for an instant losing resolution, courage or respect for duties; a woman capable of a passion that takes nothing from her virtue, takes a great deal from herself, so Theazir could not help liking her, holding her in esteem, and even sometimes feeling sorry for Kemiskir and her lover.

Both of them spent several years in that state, without the veridical mirror enabling Theazir to perceive any change in her husband's heart, nor any reason to esteem its possessor any less; that interesting article even rendered Theazir rather indifferent as to what else the mirror could tell her.

Coroes died and the prince, who had shared the weight of government with him for a long time, succeeded him, without his new occupations or his new grandeur changing anything, either of his sentiments or his fortune in the direction of amour. Having the same attachment for the sovereign as she had had for the prince, Kemiskir still had the same respect for her duties.

She did not enjoy for long the extreme consideration that she had acquired; a mortal malady came to carry her way in a matter of days; she took away the sincere regrets of all those who had known her.

The sovereign's grief was so intense, and, by virtue of a delicate concern for Theazir than he had never belied, he made so much effort to devour it in secret, that he could not sustain it for long without falling victim to it. All the secrets of the art could only prolong his life for six months after the loss of Kemiskir.

The queen honored the memory of her husband with tears that time could not dry up; she regretted equally having lost him and not having possessed his heart while he was alive; that privation, of which nothing had been able to take the place, from the instant that she had sensed it had changed her character completely. Without appearing sad to any excess, she had always been serious, although her fundamental humor and turn of mind inclined her to joviality. Throughout her life, however, which was long, she possessed the esteem and love of her subjects, and received the marks of their attachment and their respect until the very end.

After her, the enchanted mirror passed successively over the dressing tables of a numerous succession of princesses of her blood and of her family; it did not break in the hands of any. Whatever care has been taken to consult the anecdotes and secret memoirs of the court, it has not been possible to learn anything certain about the detail of the events in favor of which the mirror was conserved from Theazir all the way to Princess Amasie, whose story is found entire and coherently enough in very curious secret memoirs.

The interval separating those two princesses being several centuries, it would be rather difficult, in such a long time, for a denouncer as exact and as true as the mirror not to give rise to many singular facts and events whose description might be amusing ad even instructive, so it is a genuine loss, but as it is irreparable, it is necessary to reconcile oneself to it, and to be content with the story that will follow in the second part.

PART TWO

In those early times, so remote that hardly any trace of them remains visible, when apish old enchanters and wizened little fays made a pastime of endowing innocent creatures who had been incomparably beautiful without those superfluous gifts with every ugliness, or raising invincible obstacles to the happiness of those they had been unable to uglify, always addressing princesses and queens in order to make such stupid presents without having any other reason than some quibble—a petty failure of politeness like not writing to invite them to a wedding or a childbirth or not having offered them the first chair or the first bouquet—those times that we only know via the veritable stories that remain to us, it appears from a few examples, rather rare in truth, that enchanters and fays, in spite of their wands, giants, steel castles and all the apparatus of magic, would have been rather insignificant individuals if our true hobgoblins—which is to say, our passions—had not given them abundant aid.

In fact, those princes who went forth and were caught in a snare, to be enchanted, to sleep or be metamorphosed for two or three hundred years, were always proud crackbrains who wanted to traversed lakes of fire; to cleave giants, or dragons whose breath was sulfurous and scales brazen; to pierce towers of bronze or diamond; all with swords that would have broken against a fir-hedge. The princesses who were abducted, uglified and the rest were no more reasonable; they had always wanted to take the air at undue hours; they had separated from their followers in a wood or on the sea shore in order to dream about some unknown prince; and when the fault was committed and the enchanter or the rival fay had put in a cage or uglified the silly goose who had taken the risk, she could do nothing better than weep methodically for her liberty or her lost beauty, which renders neither one nor the other.

But let us forget all those illustrious unfortunates, who asked for it, and of whom we are only making mention in order to make it evident how superior to them Princess Amasie was, by virtue of the use she made of the fatal mirror placed in her family by the enchanter Mirzaf.

It was destined by that ridiculous and vindictive lover to trouble the repose of all the princesses descended from Narbe who possessed it. It became in Amasie's hands a torch that illuminated without ever leading astray, because her reason had sufficient mastery over her passions to render her superior to all enchantments.

She owed the light of day Princess Almenares, and to the famous H'ydaspes, one of the greatest princes who governed Persia, but she had lost, almost at birth, the most precious advantage that the good fortune of being born to virtuous and distinguishes parents can procure, that of being formed under their eyes and upon their examples. H'ydaspes died two days after Amasie was born; she was still in early infancy when she lost her mother. Heiress of their immense Estates, she was incapable of governing them at an age when she was not even aware of them. The guardianship of the princess and the government of the realm were deferred by the unanimous suffrage of the nation to the sage Krantor, her uncle.

That prince, who was at an advanced age, possessed eminently the first of the qualities necessary to govern men: he knew them, and combined with abundant experience and knowledge a probity proof against anything. No one was therefore more capable than him of governing the State and supervising the education of a process who was its sovereign and its hope.

He made the latter point his principal affair, and sometimes said, in jest—for he was not one of those scholarly sages whose seriousness renders sagacity and scholarship equally sad—that when he had been occupied every day with what concerned his niece's education, he amused himself and relaxed thereafter in the various councils, where it was only a matter of deciding affairs of government.

As soon as Amasie was at an age to receive instruction, Krantor occupied himself entirely with the care of instructing her; the unique object of his lessons was to render the heart of his pupil, which as naturally very good, even better. He thought that the perfect goodness of the heart is the sole desirable quality in princes, worth as much on its own as all the others, which renders them great and veritably dear to those who depend on them.

"Grandeur of sentiments, elevation of intelligence, charm, penetration and a thousand other things," he said, "princes acquire without care and without precepts; everything that surrounds them contributes to instructing them and forming them in every way, but alas, everything that surrounds them does not contribute at all to augmenting within them the goodness of the heart; on the contrary, that circle works from an early hour and relentlessly to adulterate that very necessary and very precious goodness."

The lessons that had that object did not consist at all on Krantor's part of words and maxims, of which the memory often has sole charge; he only showed to the eyes of his pupil telling facts, real examples of all the virtues. He gave her mind scope to reflect and her heart to ignite over those facts and examples; it was always by means of the justice of reflections and the degree of the warmth of the sentiments that he had produced in her that he judged the progress of his lessons.

He also wanted the household of the princess to be composed of only a small number of women; he only admitted them on very singular conditions. There were never more than two, or three at the most, who were permitted to speak before the princess, and in order not to impose on those who had to be perpetually in her presence a condition that was too harsh, or even impossible, and yet to ensure that they did not fail in it, Krantor had imagined the expedient of choosing mutes. All the women who, by virtue of their functions and their estate relative to Amasie might naturally have common ideas and scantly elevated sentiments, were prevented by that means from making them appear. The guardian demanded of them, in order to admit them to the presence of his ward, not proofs of discretion but the impossibility of speech, because he regarded as very dangerous the inspirations and notions that the familiarity of subalterns might communicate to the great in the frailty of infancy.

Otherwise, the household and the society of Amasie were composed of all scholars and virtuous men in the realm, of whatever age and condition they were; knowledge and virtue were the sole titles necessary to be admitted to it, and as the taste and qualities of the person who governs becomes the spur and the model of those who are governed, savant and virtuous men were soon great in number in Persia.

Wanting them all to contribute equally to the instruction and amusement of their sovereign, Krantor named every day those who were to serve her, in such a fashion that in the course of a year she only saw the same individuals again two or three times; and in receiving from them, without perceiving it, the different genres of education proportionate to her age, she learned at the same time to know all the people of merit in her realm; she was already fifteen years old, when she had not yet conversed except with modest and communicative science, and with amiably virtues devoid of crudity. Vices, passions and ridicules had not yet approached her, and had not yet appeared to her eyes; she was unaware that society was populated by fops, perverts and monsters who only have a supportable external surface. Fortunate ignorance!

Krantor had also adopted an invariable practice; he wanted to be the first and last person who spoke to Princess Amasie every day. The evening visit contained the detail of what she had learned during the day, and the judgment she had made of the people she had seen. That recapitulation served the prince to rectify his niece's ideas, in proportion to her capacity and her strength.

The morning visit was destined to retrace and develop for her the principles of virtue, generosity and grandeur of soul of which he imagined she might have occasion to make use in the course of the day.

Furthermore, without Amasie ever having been informed of it, for as long as she was under Krantor's tutelage, there was a person hidden in the apartments she occupied, in order to write down all her statements and all her more or less accurate responses, so that the prince, when he saw her in the evening, knew everything that he had to say to her, and knew minutely the progress of her reason and the fruits of the indefatigable cares he took to render his pupil more perfect.

This is what an education so singular produced on a heart and mind equally prepared to respond to it. Scarcely was Amasie at the age when the most important occupation of persons of her sex is making sure that their dolls do not lack anything that, without passing through the dry and repellant apparatus that accompanies lessons, she had learned everything that one does not learn by wanting expressly to learn it: that which one is poorly shown by the express profession of showing.

She had collected and harvested everything useful and solid, and also everything amiable and brilliant of sciences, arts, talents rid of the dryness and pettiness of practices and methods that masters do not spare anyone because they have passed through it themselves in order to learn; they have left a sort of imprint on them that characterizes them, for the most part, and which each of them tries to communicate to his pupils as if it formed part of the art or science he is teaching.

Amasie had nothing of all that; she had the most upright, the best, the most noble and the greatest heart that one could desire in a great princess, with the most elevated genius, the most cultivated and most ornamented mind; in brief, internally, she was the most amiable person in the world.

But it is necessary to depict the exterior; the interior is doubtless the nobler and more essential portion of a person, but how the exterior interests, decides and occupies! In relation to the common run of humans, the interior resembles the necessary and the exterior the superfluous; it is the latter that one adores, desires and procures, at the expense of the former, which one overlooks, neglects and almost renounces in favor of the dear superfluity.

The private memoirs of Amasie's time make such a singular portrait of her entire person that, in order not to appear to be falling into contradiction and poor arrangement in that genre, one is obliged to admit that they are being copied word-for-word:

"Amasie sings better and has a more beautiful voice than any heard thus far in Persia. The sound of her voice, even in talking, has a softness and a harmony by which the soul is intensely moved. Her stature is tall, lithe, re-laxed and noble to the highest degree; the best made women of the court cease to appear so as soon as one sees her. Her stature alone attracts and fixes all eyes by virtue of an invincible charm; what a pity that the princess is not beautiful."

Not to displease the Persian memoirs, but this is soon said: the voice and the stature are, hover, two articles of consequence, which can repair many defects in the face. Let us follow the memoirs.

"The outline of the face of the princess is a slightly elongated oval; her forehead is majestic, her nose aquiline; her hair is black and her skin less white than brown. That ensemble does not form anything that charms and interests at the first glance; although her eyes are large, and might perhaps be beautiful if they were animated by the desire to please, they are often distracted, always indifferent; they are only employed in seeing and never in what can, on the part of a young woman, properly be called gazing. Her mouth is neither well nor poorly formed, but it is unable to laugh without a subject and to show the beautiful teeth with which it is ornamented. The result is that none of Amasie's features have anything disagreeable or repulsive individually, but as that is not sufficient to be beautiful, Amasie is not. She does not care about that and has no regret in not being—which is at least as rare as beauty itself."

On the basis of that portrait one would be tempted to believe that, if the princess was not beautiful, at least she was pretty, because, strictly speaking, there is almost no young woman on whom it does not depend to be so, when the face has nothing repellant and it is a resource that she does not neglect; but the Persian memoirs oppose that too, and continue thus:

"However easy it might be for any young person, without any beauty, at least to be pretty, Amasie is not; but that is because she does not want to be, because with care and study one knows one's graces and one's faults; one does not give either for what they really are; one exaggerates on one side and feigns, so to speak, on the other; everywhere that nature is lacking, art replaces it, by means of which one makes the most of the ensemble, and one is pretty. Amasie does not want to do any of that; she quite simply prefers not to be pretty, not to do what is necessary to appear or become so. She calls that innocent game a lie and a continual penalty. Doubtless she is wrong; on that sentiments cannot be divided.

"Over the whole of that face, such as it has just been depicted, is spread an impression of majesty, intelligence and benevolence, which form the character of the face, at the same time as they depict that of the heart. Amasie," the memoirs continue, "has moments when she seems ravishingly beautiful, when all her features, without ceasing to be themselves, take on something supernatural and divine; the princess is then more beautiful than beauty itself."

Here one is tempted to believe that the memoirs are contradictory, by virtue of that new idea of a divine beauty, which they attribute to the princess, and which is contrary to the first; but they give a satisfactory reason for that kind of contradiction.

"Amasie's beauty became dazzling at moments when she could accord some favor to those she thought worthy of obtaining one, and she was never mistaken about that. She was embellished instantly when, by means of aid or unexpected benefits, she changed the fate of someone afflicted by misfortune; then the beauty, the grandeur and the bounty of her entire soul came running to place itself on her forehead, in her eyes and on her lips; she was no longer the same person, with the same features and the same face, but a composite of all beauties united."

That is clear and just; in fact, the beauty of sentiment is independent of that of the features, and is sufficient in itself even to efface ugliness. How sweet it is only to owe one's charms to that species of make-up! When the felicity of the great consists of making the good fortune of others, opportunities for satisfaction appear underfoot at every moment; Amasie did not avoid any, with the consequence that she was often ornamented by the singular beauty that owes everything to the temper of the heart, and which is proportionate to its excellence.

The sentiments that she inspired then were more vivid than those of amity and more durable than those of amour; they were stronger than those of respect, esteem and gratitude; they were a composite of all those sentiments united. They enchained by bonds that it was impossible to break; perhaps no accomplished beauty ever causes as much passion and obtains such an empire over hearts and minds; perhaps no beauty presumes less upon them, not flattering as much the temeritous hopes of some and not discouraging as much the timid homages of others.

Amasie was always mistress of herself to such a extent that no shadow of a preference, indiscreetly or too lightly escaped, ever told anyone that his face, his behavior—in brief, his merit, whatever it might be—pleased her more than the merit of another. She never gave evidence to certain subjects disgraced by nature or accidents that she was struck by, or even aware of, their disgrace.

That quality is much rarer than one might think; it merits an explanation; it is such that it brings out the others that one has and can tarnish those one has not; it is the unique means that a woman can employ to please without exception, and at any age. The simplest commoner who possesses that gift rises above her estate and her rank; the circle to which she was destined expands and is ennobled; everyone that composes it is in accord in serving her; everything concurs in her elevation, in her good fortune; she is not a commoner, she is a kind of sovereign, whose empire extends over all hearts.

If it is a princess who possesses that gift, it makes her a divinity; but in order to possess it veritably, it requires a superior merit; everything deceives and betrays a mediocre woman of that genre, and her efforts are reduced to believing that she is doing what she is incapable of doing.

Monsieur de La Bruyère,[9] that excellent critic who knows the coverts of our heart so well, says somewhere that a man who is not certain whether he is changing, whether he is growing old, can consult the eyes of any young woman he approaches, and the tone in which she speaks to him will tell him what he dreads to know. It is, therefore, only too true that those involuntary distinctions and imperceptible preferences commonly escape us, perhaps mechanically, the effect of which is to make the bearer of an uninteresting or disgraced face sense the weight of disfavor that is attached to it; whereas a fop, a fashionable man, the idol and scourge of a circle, receives from us a kind of tribute, for which he gives us no credit, that which ought to be divided.

None of those misplaced distinctions ever escaped Princess Amasie. Accustomed since her most tender youth, by a daily commerce with men of letters and scholars of every species, to encounter people of eminent knowledge and superior merit with faces often plain and sometimes repulsive—for it must be agreed that knowledge is not incompatible with such faces—she had learned not to be seduced by the surface and not to allow herself to be dazzled by the most brilliant appearances. The consequences was that in approaching her, there was no arrogant individual, however intrepid he might be, whose conceit was not lowered and who did not feel reduced to the level and tone of everyone else. The remarks and glances of the princess were as many counterweights destined to lower some and elevate others, in proportion to the need of each.

---

[9] Jean de La Bruyère (1645-1696), author of a classic set of scathing character-studies of his contemporaries, *Caractères* (1688).

The weak and the small felt sustained and delivered of a species of oppression that they experienced everywhere else. Those who had imperfections, bodily defects that made them stand out, believed on quitting her that they no longer had them, so convinced were they that those defects had not made their ordinary impression on her.

What a fashion of obliging ugliness! What a relief for deformity! What goodness! And what gratitude it inspires! How sincerely those unaccustomed to those favors sing the praises of those from whom they receive them.

Such was Amasie, and such you are in our day, you who have forbidden me to name you, and whose sentiment and taste will easily be recognized. The only difference between you and my Amasie is the charms that make you adored owe nothing to the beauty of your soul; they only prove that a more beautiful soul cannot inhabit a more beautiful body; you are always beautiful and the Asiatic princess was only beautiful at times.[10]

Amasie was entering her fifteenth year when she was put in possession of the enchanted mirror, which had been so deadly until then to the princesses who had possessed it. Under the philosophical eyes of Amasie, however, it caused no disastrous revolutions; it did not

_____

[10] The addressee of this curious passage could be assumed to be dedicatee of the work, if she were not, in fact, named in the dedication as the Marquise de Pompadour. Perhaps the addition of the name was a late afterthought, added after the completion of the text, or perhaps the author really does have someone else in mind as a model for Amasie that she cannot name.

bring any sensible change in her ideas or her conduct with those whose interior was revealed to her.

In truth, that mirror had few occasions to speak, because the princess had no liking for those long, mute and delightful conversations that subsist and are repeated every day between a mirror and every feature of a face; everything was said between her and her mirror in an instant, with the result that few people were exposed to its denunciations. If hazard brought someone to it, the usage that the princess made of it was to warn them about the inconveniences and dangers that might follow from what she had learned; to serve secretly and surely those who had need of it; and to facilitate the triumph of virtue, the success of reason and sentiment without humiliating the passions and without making vice blush, which she took equal care to hide and punish.

The first news that the veridical mirror conveyed to her concerned Nerika, one of the prettiest ladies of the court. She found herself in an embarrassing situation, not with regard to her past virtue, of which the mirror spoke very well, but the present, about which she had anxieties. She had pawned all her jewelry in order to honor a sacred engagement; it was a gambling debt. Her husband, intractable on such an article, was beginning to have some suspicion of it and was pressing her to display it.

Galaor, the superintendent of state tributes, an old libertine of immense wealth, informed of Nerika's embarrassment, had conceived the design to profit from it. He had adroitly offered her the ten thousand pieces of gold she needed in order to retrieve the diamonds, and had offered them on conditions that the pressing circumstance had caused her not to reject outright, and which she was on the point of accepting. She had agreed to meet Galaor in an isolated grove of trees that evening, in order to speak to him as his ideas merited and, make him understand that it was impossible to have the slightest obligation to him.

An hour before that of the rendezvous, Amasie wrote this note to Nerika:

Galaor will not go to the grove; a woman as discreet as she is generous, to whom he is sacrificing you and who scorns him abundantly, is sending you your diamonds; amity serves better and has fewer expense than amour; do not gamble any longer on your word, or only make confidence of your losses to veritable friends.

That gesture made all the impression on Nerika that was due; she was fearful, and desired in vain to discover to whom she was obliged for the diamonds and the advice by which they were accompanied. She did not gamble again, and when Galaor, who had been kicking his heels in the grove, wanted to enter into clarifications and justifications, he was received with so much indignation and scorn that he was ashamed. Nerika continued to be virtuous and pretty.

Two charming young people also experienced the treason of the mirror and Amasie's aid. One was Phaal, Krantor's page; he was scarcely fourteen years old; his face was such that the imagination of the best painters would have given it to Amour; no one was more interesting or more accomplished. Thus, that dangerous page pleased prudes in secret and was openly enticed by coquettes; he was the object of many tender prayers and many gallant projects that he did not see because he had seen all too clearly young Oris, the daughter of the foremost of the mutes who had served Amasie in her childhood.

Oris was anything but mute; everything about her spoke and spoke well: vivacity, finesse, charm, brilliant intellect, grace, talent and piquant beauty; she combined everything and was only thirteen; she was a prodigy. The two children loved one another furiously; they had never told one another so, for want of being able to talk to one another, because Oris's mother was her shadow, but they had found a means of writing so much that they had finally decided to run away together.

Hazard determined that on the day they had marked for the ceremony of their escape that Krantor charged his favorite page with taking the princes a basket of rare flowers that she had requested. It was the first time that Phaal had been honored by such a marked distinction. Amasie was at her dressing-table; he approached her as far as the distance indicated to him by Oris's mother, put one knee on the floor and presented her with the basket with all the appropriate respect and grace.

His face, which competed with the flowers that he had come to offer, formed a tableau whose mild voluptuousness was communicated to the entire circle of women that surrounded Amasie. He was about to extract himself from it marvelously when Oris emerged precipitately from a cabinet to Amasie's right, her eyes lowered upon a case of diamonds that she was bringing to the princess in order for her to choose those she wanted to employ for her adornment.

Oris, contemplating the diamonds to the right of the princess, while Phaal was holding the basket of flowers to her left, formed an admirable pendant with her, without her perceiving it. Scarcely had Oris raised her eyes than her blush and her disturbance commenced to betray her. As for Phaal, he was struck to such a degree on seeing her appear that, pale and tottering on his knees, he dropped the basket and the flowers were strewn at Amasie's feet. Oris, who was the first to perceive the state that her lover was in, was not the mistress of her fright; she uttered a dolorous cry and dropped the diamonds, which ran to mingle with the flowers.

It was at that moment that Amasie, seeing both of them in the mirror, learned of their amour, the commerce of their letters, their project of running away, the means, the preparations, the execution and the consequences. That singular chatterbox said more in the blink of an eye than it was possible to learn elsewhere in two hours of consecutive conversation.

The consequences would be terrible for Phaal; the palace of the princesses of Persia was an inviolable refuge; any species of offense against the honor of those who inhabited it was punishable by death; neither the youth of the abductor nor the favor of the prince he served would have been able to save him. Amasie was frightened by the danger into which the two children were about to hurl themselves.

Phaal was of an illustrious birth, but devoid of fortune. Oris was of an extraction far inferior to that of her lover, but she had considerable wealth. There are lands where those disproportions form conveniences that draw people closer; that was not the case in Persia, with the consequence that the lovers could not hope to be united by the consent of their families, but both were absolutely dependent on the princes they served until their twentieth year. In truth, it was without example for the princes to make use of that right to dispose before that age of those whose masters they were, but Amasie thought that the circumstance could dispense with the ordinary rules.

She informed Krantor of the discoveries she had made and the resolution she had formed to unite a couple so worthy of being happy and so ready to doom themselves. The prince consented to what his niece requested of him; Oris was ennobled and Phaal's fortune was assured without them being informed of it.

Meanwhile, Amasie, who wanted to punish both of them before fulfilling their wishes, arranged things in such a fashion that Oris was unable to go to the place in the gardens where Phaal was to wait for her at an appointed time at nightfall; but he did not fail to find in her stead a hideous old mute. As she was veiled, had a very similar stature to Oris and was dressed in her clothes, the amorous Phaal took her silence for the effect of dread, only thinking about getting her out of the palace gardens promptly. He had scarcely taken for steps outside the enclosure when he was seized and abducted himself, with his prey.

As soon as it was time to allow Oris her liberty, Amasie, who had kept her out of sight until that moment, dismissed her, and the impatient Oris ran to where she expected to find Phaal waiting. She only found an old negro there, disguised and masked, whom the obscurity prevented her from recognizing, and who took her in his arms, not giving her the time to distinguish the frightful difference there was between him and her lover.

Phaal, who had been separated from the person that he was abducting by those who had arrested him, was taken before Krantor; he was unaware of his misfortune and his mistake.

On seeing him, the prince said: "You have just violated the sacred refuge of the Queens of Persia; that secret is still in my power, but in a moment I will no longer be the master of it, and your life will be over. My generosity leaves you one resource and the present moment to decide; you can be taken within the hour to the Temple of the Sun to give your faith to the person you have abducted, or you can be taken to the scaffold; choose, and tell us your choice without delay."

Believing that he was about to possess his dear Oris, Phaal had no need to deliberate. Scarcely had he sworn to marry her than the veil that hid the mute woman was lifted; rage and all the horrors combined entered Phaal's heart.

The same ceremony was observed in Amasie's apartment, to which Oris and the masked negro had been taken; the responses were the same; a delighted consent was initially given by Oris to the engagement she believed at she was making with Phaal; a mortal dolor succeeded it as soon as the old negro had removed his mask and shown his face.

It was in that state that they were taken to the temple by different paths; Oris was dragged there dying, and Phaal was furious, meditating vengeances of every species. Meanwhile, the mute and the negro had disappeared and did not make the journey, but Phaal only saw the mute in the veiled Oris and the unfortunate Oris did not deign to raise her gaze toward the person she believed to be the odious negro; she turned her eyes away with horror, and he avoided her with as much fear. It was in those dispositions that they were united.

When the ceremony as over they were taken back to Amasie's palace, to which Krantor had gone in order to enjoy the surprise and the first moment of the felicity of two hearts ready to pass from a state so cruel to one so sweet.

The two lovers ran, one to Amasie's feet and the other to Krantor's knees; both requested death a thousand times over rather than living for an instant separated from the person they loved and in unions that horrified them.

Amasie, lifting up Oris benevolently, showed her by way of response her lover prostrated before Krantor; that prince, making him a sign to get up, said to him: "Recognize Oris, receive her from the hands of the Princess; be happy, both of you, by virtue of her cares, and be worthy of her generosity and mine."

Phaal, bewildered, not knowing whether he was emerging from a dream or entering into another, gazed for a long time at Oris and the princess without seeing ether of them, but when the initial shock had given way to sentiments of hope and joy, which entered into his soul in a host, he was carried away by such excesses of rapture and gratitude that one might have thought that he had lost his mind.

Amasie wanted the day to be celebrated by a gallant fête, which she imagined immediately, and of which she did the honors. Oris and Phaal owed her the happiness of their life, and always conserved the most intense gratitude to her.

Such was the usage that the princess made of the confidences of her mirror; it never spoke to her about anyone without giving her the opportunity to exercise a few virtues and performing some action worthy of her. Oppressed innocence never found any surer support, nor misfortune any help better matched to the needs of the unfortunate.

Human pride frequently makes tyrants of those who oblige, and even more frequently makes ingrates of those who are obliged; it mingles in the appreciation of gifts to exaggerate them in the eyes of the benefactor and to finish them in the eyes of the recipient of the benefit. Amasie had a sure means of avoiding that double reef; she was able to distribute her benefits with the promptitude and the secrecy that characterizes those of the divinity.

If it was a matter of deciding between two competitors, the art of supplanting, of appearing worthier, was a lost art as soon as the mirror had spoken, because the appetite of the princess for the truth did not permit her to be deceived by the intrigue, conspiracy, illusion and plotting of the court, which are so well able to injure merit, eclipse it and often to render it ridiculous.

O too useful mirror! Why have you not, hundreds of times since, enlightened those who dispense grandeurs, fortune and dignities on the earth, and who have such a great need of you in order not to be the victim of rogues and flatterers, in order not to prefer the thinnest tinsel to the purest gold; but alas, you are no more; you have been put away long ago in the furniture-store of some enchanter who no longer allows you to see the light of day.

It is by means of you that Amasie read in all hearts, fathoming their most secret recesses, without penetrating whence that knowledge came, and employed it all for the welfare of society; it by means of you that she encouraged noble and great actions, those in which she found the fortunate seeds of virtues; by means of you she reanimated legitimate hope, she smoothed out difficulties and prepared unexpected successes. With a glance or a word she spread the intimate consolations that go to dry up tears at their source, and the treasures and assistance were only inexhaustible for good people. By means of you, finally, the perverse and the perfidious, a breed emboldened and multiplied by success, found obstacles and ambushes everywhere; Amasie took delight in disconcerting them, eviscerating their ruses, destroying one by means of another; nothing succeeded for them—a strange thing; everywhere else they seemed made to prosper.

Krantor no longer had any instruction to give his ward; he contented himself with admiring her. Her actions, even more than her discourse, appeared to him, as to the entire court, to be as many examples and lessons of profound sagacity, prudence and sublime virtue. Not knowing the cause of the sure presentiment that enlightened the princess regarding the future and the interior of almost all those whom she knew, he could only attribute to the elevation of her genius, to something divine that he respected in her, as in an inspired individual. He no longer gave her advice, and did not decide anything important without taking hers and following it blindly. A few occasions when he had not thought that he ought to defer to her had not gone well, and eventuality had proved to him that Amasie saw beyond what human prudence and ordinary knowledge were able to penetrate.

Only one point mingled bitterness with the satisfaction of that prince; his infirmities and his old age no longer permitted him to flatter himself that he would live for many years. Amasie was of an age to choose a husband and to give successors to the Empire; all her subjects formed prayers for that great event, and Krantor desired it ardently. The princess was the only person who did not appear to desire it.

The neighboring princes who could aspire to that alliance had attempted in regard to Krantor all possible proposals, all the treaties advantageous to Persia and appropriate to determine him in their favor; none had succeeded.

Krantor, convinced that if he used all his authority over his niece, she would defer to it without even manifesting the slightest reluctance, even if she experienced a invincible one, was far from making use of that authority to constrain her. He wanted taste to determine her choice. However, he secretly desired that she might decide in favor of one of the sons of his old friend Nouskirvan.

That prince, whose estates neighbored Amasie's, had two sons of markedly opposed character; the elder was an intrepid warrior and nothing more, the younger a sage, a philosopher who combined useful knowledge with the solid virtues that, in a sovereign, make the felicity of the people he governs.

Thus far, Nouskirvan had employed his two sons in conformity with their character; he had made use of Thaamar to contain his subjects in their duty, to help his allies and render himself redoubtable to his enemies; that prince had always been at the head of his armies and had been victorious as many times as he had had occasion to do battle.

Zoophir had not quit Nouskirvan, and had occupied himself in making the laws respected, procuring abundance, security and tranquility in the interior of their estates, protecting the useful arts, policing mores, extending commerce and enabling it to flourish. In brief, the elder had rendered Nouskirvan's reign redoubtable and respected externally, while the younger had rendered it pleasant and fortunate internally.

That sage king would dearly have liked his two sons to be able, after him, to maintain that fortunate accord in his empire, but he foresaw that it would not subsist for long if they came to share it, because the seething martial ardor of Thaamar would incline him to vast projects beyond his strength, of which his subjects would become the victims; he thought, therefore, of leaving his estates entirely to Zoophir, but that could only be done with Thaamar's consent, by placing him on a throne capable of fulfilling all of his ambition. Zoophir had the hearts and prayers of the people, but Thaamar was the god of the army.

Nouskirvan, convinced that he could not divide his estates between two sons of such opposite character, nor leave them entirely to either of the two without exposing his real to catastrophic upheavals, regarded Persia as a theater worthy of Thaamar: immense territories, various and innumerable peoples, external wars of every sort and frequent internal disputes, were subjects to exercise the talents of that prince; and in order to place him on that throne it only required a word from Amasie. Nouskirvan flattered himself that the word in question would not be difficult to obtain, if the prince went to the Persian court to solicit it himself.

He counted on the brilliant merit of Thaamar, on the conquering ascendancy that characterized him in everything: in his face, in his actions, in his slightest gesture. Everything about him announced the prince, the hero, the man above others, in such a fashion that it was impossible, on seeing him, to be affected by another idea.

Nouskirvan even wanted Zoophir to accompany his brother, in order that his modest and philosophical simplicity would serve as a shadow to the brilliance of the elder.

Thaamar combined with the tallest, noblest and best formed stature one of those faces in which every feature is such that it is impossible to see anything more handsome, except for the ensemble; one of those faces that confuse and uglify all those that are compared with it.

As for Zoophir, he was not sculpted as a hero so much as a philosopher, not as tall, and stouter than his brother, without being badly made, his stature did not have the same liberty or the same nobility; his physiognomy was mild, intelligent and interesting, but obfuscated by the philosophical gravity that causes those sorts of faces to be examined with less attention; one is not struck by them at first, it is true that is true that once they have commenced to please they achieve it, and when they do please, it is greatly and for a long time.

The latter prince had very fine eyes, with which he saw very well at close range and very poorly at a distance—what we commonly call short sight; among us it is a demeanor, thanks to our spectacles; it is a conventional and fashionable kind of sight; in the beginning it was a kind of sign and badge of literary merit, but people have been so misled by it that it longer signifies anything except that one really is short-sighted, or pretends to be. That sort of vision was so rare in Persia in Zoophir's day that no one had imagined drawing any inference from it; it was an inconvenience, a defect, and nothing more.

At any rate, such were the two princes; their reputation and personal merit had gone before them, and they were well known in Amasie's court before they appeared there.

The public pretext for their voyage was the ratification of an ancient treaty that Nouskirvan had made with Amasie's father, and which he desired his children, ready to succeed him, to renew after him, in order to strengthen and conserve the union that had subsisted every since between the two nations. The secret motive, of which Nouskirvan had notified Krantor, was to please the princess and give by virtue of her choice a master to her Empire.

Krantor received the two princes with the distinction and the honors due to their rank. Everyone of high birth in the court was assembled in Amasie's palace when he introduced the two brothers to her; the most flattering and most select eulogies were employed respectively, with the delicate measurement and fine taste that seduces and persuades, and which is so different from the lavish and inappropriate effusion that signifies nothing, so that first meeting was one of the most fortunate there had ever been. The princes took away from it a high idea of the merit and intelligence of Amasie, and inspired in her an advantageous view of theirs.

However, the external brilliance and enchanting ascendancy of Thaamar had made the general and immediate impression that draws and subjugates without allowing deliberation, whereas the milder qualities of Zoophir had been much less striking. However sublime merit is, when it is simple and modest, one can count on it being imperceptible for a long time to the distracted gaze of the multitude; it is only sensed and appreciated by a small number of connoisseurs.

Krantor, above all, was enchanted by Thaamar; in no time at all he passed in his regard from admiration and esteem to the most tender amity: a rare sentiment, but extreme, and bindles in old age, more miserly and more incapable of amity in proportion to the diminution of the expectation of inspiring it. The same weakness that chills and dries up therein the source of its first attachments gives to new ones a sort of excess and obstinacy.

But if Krantor was charmed by the merit and face of Thaamar, Princess Amasie was even more sensitive to it; seeing him and loving him were the same thing for her; her sagacity, her reason and her indifference did not de-

fend her for an instant. Sagacity and reason are vain resources against the involuntary and absolute movement
that forces us to love: a movement swifter than lightning,
more prompt than thought; the heart alone has decided it,
a long time before the mind deliberates and the reason
can serve to regulate and constrain that movement. Often, it only serves us against it at the expense of the happiness and repose of our life.

That was the aid that got the princess out of it; she
made use of it to hide so well the sentiments against
which she had not been able to defend herself that
Thaamar was never aware of them.

That prince soon perceived the advantageous dispositions that Krantor had for him; he knew the extent to
which his choice might be decisive, and what ascendancy he had over the mind of his niece. It would not have
taken much for her to have inspired in him the sentiments that she had conceived for him, but sovereigns
regard that article as unnecessary in the treaties that unite
them. Amasie's crown flattered the ambition and projects of Thaamar; that crown had need of a support. The
sagacity of the government that Krantor and Amasie had
established left Persia nothing to desire but an arm to
defend it against its enemies, and no one was more worthy and more capable of that care than Thaamar. He
would have no difficulty in making Krantor enter into all
his views in that regard; that reason alone seemed to decide in his favor and soon formed a powerful party in the
Empire.

That strong reason was also the one of which
Krantor made use in regard to Amasie. "Your estates,"
he often said to her, "will always be sustained from
within by the affection of your people for you and your
attachment for them, by the profound wisdom with

which you are able to govern them. They know that and respect it; you will always find within yourself all the resources necessary to the maintenance of a good government in peace time; you only have need of help externally; it's in war, against your enemies, that you lack a defender, and it's a hero, it's Thaamar, who wants to be that man, and whom I propose to you."

Amasie's heart would easily have made that choice without politics giving her the advice, but the more her heart inclined her to choose thus, the less it could resolve to suffer that politics had any part in it. The princess knew, moreover, how capable Thaamar was of sustaining a great Empire; she knew only too well the hero in him, but she did not know the lover sufficiently; the more she sensed how dear to her he would become, the more interest she had in discovering whether he was capable of loving—with the result that she often replied to Krantor in a vague and indecisive fashion that did not announce to him either a negation or a disposition to determination.

She rendered justice to the virtues and gave the greatest eulogies to the merit and valor of the prince, with the secret pleasure that a sensitive and deeply touched heart savors when it can be satisfied, without betraying itself, in talking about the person it loves; but she did not appear as convinced as Krantor would have liked her to be of the need of associating a conqueror with the Empire.

She proved to him by means of many arguments and examples that warriors have more often toppled States than sustained them; that there is no government that is not strong enough and cannot find within itself the resources and bravery for a legitimate self-defense, the only kind that is just; whereas the thirst for conquest, only seeing war that is not permitted to it, is sometimes as unfortunate as it has been unmeasured.

Krantor, who could not resolve to constrain his niece, also could not doubt that she would eventually yield to the evidence, on the side of her interests, and to the merit of Thaamar, with the consequence that he advised the prince to finish by his assiduity and his attentions to Amasie what he assured him was already far advanced by the favorable dispositions he supposed the princess to have.

Thaamar did not neglect anything in order to succeed; he feigned a sensibility so delicate and so respectful, and deployed an art and graces so naïve, that Amasie might have been deceived by them. Hearts incapable of perfidy cannot suspect it in others; their candor merits assistance; Amasie's was usefully served by her faithful mirror.

At the moment when she was commencing to acquire confidence in Prince Thaamar's seductive speeches, she saw in her mirror two of the most beautiful women in the court, to whom he had made the most tender protestations on the same day. She judged by the excess to which both of them appeared seduced by them, and all that the prince had put into them of real or feigned passion in order to inspire something similar, that either he really had felt it for both of them at the same time, which would have been difficult, or that he had experienced it for neither one, which was much easier to believe.

The princess found nothing satisfying in either of those alternatives; the character of Thaamar appeared to her to be false and dangerous, and only announced consequences for her as sad for her delicacy as for her penchant.

Two days later, there was a new confidence on the mirror's part. A young woman of exquisite beauty found herself interested and compromised in almost the same fashion as the other two; the mirror even said something a little stronger against her. The next day, a further report, against two of the foremost ladies of the court, both very beautiful, each utterly enchanted by Thaamar, each utterly convinced personally that she was loved uniquely.

Every day procured Amasie discoveries of the same sort, with the result that in very little time she could no longer doubt that all the lovely women in the court were in intrigue and in relation with the prince, and that all of them had had the weakness to believe him, having been deceived in the same fashion, the only difference being in the degree; some had believed him too much, and the mirror had no difficulty in saying so; there was every appearance that the less credulous would reach the same state as the others with time.

Thus, Amasie, no longer able to esteem Thaamar, was reduced to wanting to hate him; but that cruel sentiment is not born in us by desire, and we are perhaps never further way from it than when we form the wish.

Meanwhile, the more the prince affected in her regard sentiments by which she could not believe him really to be touched, the more she was wounded by it, without making it appear. Her dolor was sharper in proportion to his ability to employ more adroitly the colors of truth in order to deceive her.

Might he not in fact be as he wants to appear to me to be, or why is he so well able to appear to be what he is not? she often asked herself, after having heard him. *No, Amasie is too true to be the victim of imposture; he will never know how much I would have loved him, since*

I know too well how unworthy he is of my tenderness incapable of responding to it sincerely.

That conduct on the part of the prince caused Krantor to lose all the fruits of the accurate reasoning that he did not weary of employing with regard to Amasie. He could not conceive how it was possible that he made such little progress in an affair where all political advantages and all personal charms were united. He saw all of that in Thaamar, and he was right but he did not see what the mirror was able to oppose to so many advantages and charms.

It was necessary, therefore, to resolve to expect everything of the merit and passion of the prince with which Krantor was quite satisfied and quite convinced. Thaamar himself, no longer counting on anything else, had no less good an opinion of his success; supposing its infallibility in advance, his self-esteem was no less flattered by it.

But it is time to return to Zoophir, of whom we have completely lost sight since his arrival in Persia. Although his debut there appeared less brilliant and less fortunate than that of Thaamar, his reputation was solidly established, and it was augmented every day, to such a degree that, in the measure that Thaamar lost ground in the heart of the princess, Zoophir took possession of it with his intellect.

All the sages and scholars of every sort who were then making the honor of Persia respected the knowledge and the enlightenment of the prince, and rendered him the sincere homage that only the superiority of science and genius could obtain from those proud Republicans, who recognized no other elevation or empire in that genre. It was by that entitlement that Zoophir, enjoying the esteem of all the sages and scholars in Persia, soon acquired all of Amasie's.

In the circles composed of those men, who assembled every day at a fixed hour in Amasie's palace, she soon remarked that nothing was obscure, difficult or hidden for the prince; that everywhere that the enlightenment and penetration of his genius spread light and enabled unknown verities to shine, it was with as much force and clarity as charm and mildness. She shared, therefore, with all the philosophers and savants of her Empire, the sentiment of admiration and veneration that they had conceived for him. That sentiment, when it is pure and devoid of envy on the part of savants, is a kind of worship; it produces the most flattering and most profound respect that exists on the earth.

Such was Zoophir in Persia; but, accustomed to that homage, as a tribute that his knowledge and his genius had attracted to him everywhere, he was neither proud of it not flattered by it. He was uniquely sensitive to the sentiments of Amasie, because he had conceived for her all those of which Prince Thaamar could only affect the appearance, and the savant, the unfortunate sage, hid them dolorously, devoured them in secret in the depths of his heart, while the fickle warrior displayed publicly the shadow and the surface of them.

Amasie was far from suspecting in Zoophir a passion that he hid with all the care of which he was capable. If she had divined it, it would have been one pain more. It is as sad to inspire tender sentiments in those one esteems veritably, to which one cannot respond, as it is to sense that one cannot inspire them.

But without loving those by whom one is perfectly loved, without knowing it, without even desiring it, what their heart hides nevertheless operates upon ours in secret. It affects it and interests it in such a manner that the indifference we believe that we have for them does not resemble that which we really have for those who are perfectly indifferent to us.

Amasie experienced that on seeing Zoophir; she had known the beauty of his genius in public conferences in which the prince always appeared to have new advantages; a secret impulse caused her to desire to know his heart and his character in private conversations; and those private conversations led her to esteem him even more by the heart than by the mind; to have the most entire confidence in him, of which she was glad to give him, at every opportunity, the most marked evidence. How interesting and cruel at the same time that evidence was for a lover of Zoophir's temper; in attaching him further, it could only augment his torment.

The prince was informed of the projects and hopes of Thaamar as well as the designs of Nouskirvan, the views of Krantor and the desires of the Persians, who were all inclined toward Thaamar. He did not know what the sentiments of the princess were for his brother, already excessively fortunate in uniting so many suffrages, but even if he could have believed Amasie to be insensible to the charms of Thaamar, how could he think that he might be able to obtain from her sentiments that that prince had not been able to inspire? Was it in his simple and modest character to flatter himself thus?

Even if he had conceived the hope of it, would it have been appropriate to his sagacity to overturn so many projects, to attract so many enemies to himself: Nouskirvan, Thaamar, Kantor and the entire aristocracy of the nation? Zoophir was, therefore, firmly resolved to love without saying anything, and to suffer mortally without complaining, whatever occasions he might have to talk about it incessantly.

That mute character soon became more difficult for him to sustain.

Nouskirvan, informed by Thaamar of the extreme confidence that Amasie had in Zoophir, did not fail to charge him to employ in his brother's favor all the influence that he might have over the mind of the princess. Thaamar made him the same entreaties continually, and Krantor, with the same views, contrived frequent opportunities for him to converse with Amasie in private; and as she did not avoid any of them, Zoophir, incapable of betraying the interests most contrary to his heart, was reduced to conversing with the adored object in favor of a rival all the more dangerous because he was a rival overtly, with the support of all those in whom Amasie depended, whereas Zoophir was only a rival in secret, without the support of anyone.

He acquitted that dolorous commission with a care so well matched to Amasie's delicacy and sensibility; he demonstrated it so clearly, with regard to everything that could only interest her, and persuaded her so fully that the interest so dear to him, that she could not hide the secret of her heart from him for long. Hazard enabled the prince to surprise her alone in one of those moments of sensibility and dolor in which it is almost impossible to silence one's trouble and when the only prudence consists in choosing well in whom to confide.

That day had begun with a conversation between her and Krantor, who had pressed her more urgently and with less regard than he was accustomed to employ; he had quit her saying: "Thaamar wants to owe your choice to his sentiments for you, and you owe that to his merit; I want to owe it to your reason, and you owe that to my amity and my cares. We have obtained nothing, but the entire nation demands it of my amity, and I can no longer refuse it. It is up to you to spare me the displeasure of constraining you to it."

In the wake of that conversation, Thaamar had succeeded Krantor; never had the princess seen him so charming, so tender, so passionate, so true in appearance; but after a conversation so satisfying for her, so appropriate to accelerate the designs formed against her irresolution, she had gone into her dressing-room, where she had surprised a lady of her palace, who was readjusting her attire before the enchanted mirror. Why that adjustment? To run to a rendezvous where she was expected by Prince Thaamar; the mirror detailed in advance all the circumstances, which were such that the princess thought that she ought no longer to occupy herself with anything but fleeing him, and taking away from Krantor any hope of ever subjugating her to an engagement that would be the misfortune of her life.

In order to enjoy the pleasure of being afflicted alone and consulting herself freely and without witnesses—a pleasure that the great have so much difficulty procuring for themselves—she had gone down into one of the palace gardens with no followers except two mutes. Her reverie took her to an arbor, into which she went, making a sign to the mutes to wait some distance away.

Zoophir had been in that arbor for two hours, lying on the grass on the opposite side to the one by which the princess entered it; absorbed himself in the most profound reverie, he did not see her come in and was not perceived by her. Amasie sat down on a bed of grass placed in such a fashion that they were quite close to one another for a long time, with their backs turned, without knowing it.

Suddenly, however, a profound sigh and a few poorly articulated words that escape the prince caused Amasie to get up fearfully and precipitately in order to run away from a place where she had thought she was alone.

Perceiving her, Zoophir put one knee on the ground and offered her apologies for the involuntary indiscretion he had just committed in finding himself in a place where she evidently wanted to be alone, and not withdrawing when she came in. He excused himself on the grounds of the position that had prevented him from seeing her.

"It's me, Prince," she said, "who ought to reproach myself for having troubled your solitude and your reverie, but I don't know whether I've rendered you a disservice. The dolorous sigh that informed me that I was not alone has made me think that you were plunged in sad ideas; if I did not fear adding a second indiscretion to the first, I would ask you the subject of your troubles; my curiosity comes from my dread that you have experienced some secret displeasure among us."

Zoophir made use adroitly of the question that Amasie had asked him to speak to her in favor of Thaamar.

"To see Amasie," said the prince, "to obtain her esteem, is a privilege that no displeasure of any species can poison; sovereign over hearts and minds, all your subjects vie with one another to honor those whom you distinguish. They have heaped me with respect and tributes, but the esteem with which you have honored me, and of which I shall not be able to conserve too dear a memory, was the object of my reverie and my sadness.

"Nouskirvan has ordered me to employ myself with you in favor of a brother; than brother, whom I love, implores me incessantly to do so; even Krantor talks to me about nothing else; and I try to serve them. How inapt I am for that! I have done it, and perhaps more than I ought to have done. You have suffered my importunate solicitations generously, but I have sensed how futile they were. Your reason is in accord with everything that speaks in favor of Thaamar, but your heart imposes a secret and invincible obstacle to it."

"Oh, Prince," said Amasie, "do not judge my heart before knowing it; perhaps it would serve Thaamar better than my reason if I ceased to consult and listen to it."

The vivacity with which the princess had pronounced those words brought a mortal affliction to Zoophir's heart; to love without hope, to love in secret, is to love; to learn that the person one loves is prejudiced and touched in favor of another is to die.

"If I dared," he said, "to hear in favor of Thaamar what those few words only say by half, I would find him a thousand times more fortunate than I had thought, and than he has dared to flatter himself on being; for after all, he is made to please, he adores you; if you do not hate him, everything concurs with his happiness and nothing opposes it."

"Sage Zoophir," the princess said to him, "I do not want to, nor can I, hide my sentiments and my troubles from you any longer; it is from your counsel that I expect the help of which my reason has need, against Thaamar, against myself; I loved him as soon as I saw him; everything that Krantor has repeated to me a hundred times in his favor, everything that Nouskirvan and he have charged you with saying to me, my heart had said to me in the first instant; but that prince, who might have been my happiness if he had merited my tenderness, has rendered himself unworthy of it by virtue of everything that can wound a true and sensitive heart."

She told him then, in lengthy detail, everything that she had learned about the prince's intrigues—which were innumerable—after which she added; "Now, Zoophir, tell me that your brother adores me; tell me whether he will ever be capable of loving me as I believe that I merit being loved, and, in sum, whether I must immolate to reasons of State, or even to my penchant, all the repose of my life. Doubtless you do not know, very sage and very fortunate Zoophir, all the misfortune and torment of loving without the hope of being loved; but I, whom Thaamar has taught only too well to know him, am sure that the heart cannot experience anything more cruel, and which nothing can cure. That prince, whom I loved, and who has not loved me at all, whom perhaps I still love, and who will never love me, will not, therefore, be my husband. Help me to hate him, or at least to forget him, if that is possible; rid me adroitly, and without compromising me, of the importunate solicitations of Nouskirvan and Krantor, and all those who only see what seems to bring us together, and who do not know what separates us; keep faithfully a secret that would never have emerged from my heart, if yours had not appeared to me to be the only one worthy of my complete confidence."

If the princess had looked at Zoophir while speaking thus, she would have read on his face the impressions and the emotions of dolor and joy, which succeeded one another and destroyed one another mutually in his soul. To be chosen by the beloved object for a confidant of all the passion that a rival inspires—what torture! But also, what a relief to learn that that rival is unaware of the sentiments of which he has not been able to render himself worthy, and that nothing will bring two hearts together that are not made to be united.

The prince's joy would have been more intense and more malign if he had been capable of profiting from the confidences that Amasie had made him to do Thaamar a disservice, as she seemed to be inviting him to do; perhaps he would have succeeded had he been capable of making the attempt, but his heart was too honest to do that.

He did not speak for some time, as if buried in a profound reverie, after which he said to the princess: "No, Thaamar has not been able to see you, to hear you and know you without loving you; an excess of delicacy and sensibility have caused your alarms, but Heaven preserve me from ever trying to aid you to hate him or forget him. I would not succeed in that, and I would serve you both badly; sooner or later he will know that you love him, and how could he help adoring you then?

"All that I can see now is that I no longer have anything to say to you in favor of the prince; I cannot reveal anything to him of what you have confided to me, so I must be equally useless to both of you; however, he will demand from me solicitations that I can no longer make, and perhaps he will impute their lack of success to me. You will expect equally futile advice from me, which I cannot give you without betraying him. My condition would be too violent to be sustainable. Find it good that I go to rejoin Nouskirvan right away; Thaamar's destiny can only be fortunate, but his happiness is still distant, and my presence in our Estates has been necessary for a long time. The pretext of my health, which is deteriorating here, authorizes a departure too long delayed. Remember Zoophir sometimes as the man who desires the happiness of Amasie more than anyone else in the world."

"I believe you, Prince," Amasie said, "but I demand that you give me the most sensible evidence of it by remaining in my court, of which you are the honor and the delight, for as long as Prince Thaamar remains here. I have told you that I loved him, but I have also told you that I could not esteem him; you know the extent to which I respect and honor you; your presence will support his, and when it is necessary to lose you his absence will soften yours."

Those orders were too flattering and too precise; they were, in any case, too much in conformity with Zoophir's secret inclination for him to defend himself against them. He only responded with a profound bow, and, presenting his hand to the princess, he escorted her back to the palace.

That first conversation was followed by a number of others, in which Amasie, enabled Zoophir to see how capable she was of loving, and how worthy she was of being loved. The prince's passion was augmented to such an excess that, in making an extreme effort to hide it, beyond his strength, his health was attacked dangerously; a mortal sadness, a languor that increased every day, soon caused anxiety for his life; all the medicaments and care of which the art is capable were exhausted without success. The maladies whose source is in the heart only receive consolation from the heart itself.

"What chagrin is consuming and devouring you in our midst?" Amasie often said to him. "Why are you hiding it from me? Can it be, Prince, that my confidence has not been able to obtain yours for me? Flee a foreign, hostile land; our gods are deaf to the prayers that I say for you; go implore those of your homeland; I consent to it; it is too long to deprive Nouskirvan of a son who must be so dear to him—but in what state is Persia sending back that son!"

"Don't impute the languor that is killing me," the prince said, "to the fortunate climate in which you live, to the pure and mild air which one breathes near you, or to chagrins that I want to hide from you for lack of confidence. To what is it due, then? Life, health, the mechanisms destined to conserve one and the other are so fragile! They deteriorate in so many fashions. If the number of days that ought to shine for me is ready to be accomplished, let the last one commence and finish next to Amasie, in swearing that those I have passed there have been the most beautiful of my life."

She was so touched by the poor state in which she saw the prince, that the sentiments he expressed had as much truth as tenderness. Attributing them solely to esteem and amity, she admired their character and strength.

Why, she said to herself sometimes, *has Thaamar not conceived for me the same amity that renders his brother so sensitive to everything that concerns me? It seems to me that I would be contented, that it would at least have repaid and justified all the attachment that he had inspired in me, instead of which I am repaying Zoophir's amity poorly; I pity him, I interest myself in his languor, but not with the tender vivacity that he affects for me, and I reproach myself for it.*

But that error of the princess regarding the sentiments of Zoophir, or rather, their true motive, was about to cease, and Thaamar was to give birth to the occasion,

He was very smitten with a young foreigner named Liga, who had not been with Amasie long. The difficulty of seeing her in the palace, entry to which was only free to him at certain hours, made him imagine the expedient of having her emerge in the evening in the costume of one of the slaves who worked in the gardens. The inexperienced Liga, not knowing all the danger to which she was exposing herself, made two or three attempts, which succeeded, but one arrived that doomed her; she was recognized and arrested. The disguise itself was a capital crime, treated as high treason, on the part of anyone resident inside the palace. The quality of foreigner aggravated Liga's crime further.

She was put in irons; her execution would have followed swiftly if Thaamar, who was informed of it, had not had recourse to Zoophir. He implored him and pressed him so strongly to obtain mercy for an innocent about to perish, and Zoophir was so touched by the indiscretion to which his brother had reduced her, that he could not help making the attempt.

He did more; he resolved to take responsibility personally for Thaamar's fault and to take upon himself everything that Amasie might imagine regarding that disguise. He knew her sensitivity for everything relating to the real guilty party, and made it a delicate pleasure to spare that blow to a woman in love who already had too much of which to complain, and who would be wounded in addition.

Anxious about the eventuality and fearing that his brother's entreaties might not be sufficiently forceful, Thaamar wanted to accompany him, in order to be a witness and to join his own with them. Zoophir consented to that, and as there was not a moment to lose, he used for the first time the liberty that Krantor had given him to enter Amasie's palace at any hour of the day.

She was still in bed; the princes were introduced into her cabinet to wait until the hour when she was dressed; it was the first time since their arrival in Persia that they had had occasion to appear before the terrible avenging mirror, which enlightened Amasie so perfectly without her being aware of it.

She made them wait for some time. Zoophir, distressed and dejected, scarcely able to stand up, had the courage to accuse himself, to provide the imaginary detail of a adventure in which he had no part, and concluded his story by imploring mercy for Liga. Candor was painted on his forehead, and death on his lips.

Thaamar dared to joining his entreaties with those of his brother, and, believing himself to be exempt from suspicion, he put brilliance and grace thereinto, when he ought only to have employed repentance and shame.

But what wasted lies! The hearts of the two brothers were uncovered; their souls were naked for Amasie before the mirror. What a contrast! What a tableau for her! What singular and redoubled blows!

What a heart, in her eyes, was that of Zoophir: of Zoophir dying, and dying voluntarily for her, for the most tender, vivid passion, perfect and true, hidden thus far with so much care and courage. How worthy he appeared of being pitied—or, rather, of being loved!

But how Thaamar, uniquely occupied with the care of deceiving her, in order to satisfy his ambition, showed himself to be vile and despicable in her eyes!

Buried in a sea of astonishment and reflections, she remained motionless for some time, save for her eyes, the gaze of which moved alternately between the two princes and the mirror. The silence was only interrupted by the order to bring Liga before her. Thaamar shivered at that, in the dread of what her responses to Amasie's questions might do to him, by revealing what he believed to be hidden. He wanted to say a few words in order to deter that order, but the princess made him a sign to remain silent, and reentered into the abyss of her own thoughts until the moment when Liga appeared.

Then, resuming the free and majestic air that characterized her in everything, and which she had only been seen to lose on this occasion, Amasie said to Zoophir. "Prince, discretion and grandeur of soul have limits; you have surpassed them, even at the expense of life; it is time to put them in order; I am taking responsibility for that care. I believe that I would be offending you in granting you Liga's mercy; it is to Prince Thaamar that it is due, and it is to him alone that I give it; it is the only one that he will obtain from me. You, Zoophir, remember, that from this moment on, there are no longer any favors that Amasie can refuse you."

Scarcely had she finished speaking than she disappeared, leaving the two princes equally astonished by what they had just heard.

Thaamar found that what related to him was so clearly expressed that he did not waste time reflecting in order to penetrate its meaning. Fully convinced that he was doomed without resource with regard to Amasie, he turned all his hopes toward Krantor and the nobles who formed a party in his favor. He flattered himself that authority and intrigues might be able to bring back, or at least constrain, the princess, and that there was not a moment to lose in making use of them—with the consequence that he ran to render an account of what he had just hard to Krantor, and to deliberate with him and those who desired his elevation to the throne as to the measures to be taken to oblige Amasie to place him on it.

As for Zoophir, his trouble and astonishment were boundless; he could not doubt that Amasie was informed of everything that he had tried to hide, regarding the adventure of Liga, by means of an obliging lie in favor of his brother. Supposing her to be informed on that point, she had had reason to say to him that grandeur of soul has limits and that he had surpassed them, but why speak to him about discretion? Why tell him that he had surpassed the bounds of that? That he was on the point of losing his life thereby? Why add that it was time to put that in order, and that she would take responsibility for it?

How could that be understood except by supposing that Amasie had finally penetrated the secret of his heart, that she knew all the passion by which he was devoured, and was ready to perish for having wanted too much and having tried too hard to hide it? But how? He was certain of having hidden it well, of not having confided it to anyone whatsoever.

Would a princess so accurate, so measured in all her expression, have spoken in such a precise fashion about what she had only divined from conjectures? No, undoubtedly, it was necessary that she was certain of it, and that she knew Zoophir's heart better than he did; the care for which she wanted to take responsibility was proof of it; it could not signify anything other than that she was sensitive to his passion, that she wanted to respond to it. How could he dare to believe it? But how was he able to doubt it?

What a day! What hope began to shine in the depths of his bewildered heart! Unable to banish those excessive flattering ideas, and not daring to liberate himself from them, suspended between the horror of self-deception and the charm of hope, his health was only further deteriorated by the continual agitation of his mind.

For her part, Amasie was penetrated by the conviction and the interior impression made on her by the verities that the mirror had revealed, although she attributed everything that she learned by that means to an infallible inspiration that she had at certain moments, and did not have the faintest idea that the mirror had anything to do with it. No longer doubting Zoophir's extreme passion, and knowing all its force and extent, she could not weary of admiring the discretion and the courage with which he had sustained the crushing confidences that she had made him and the cruel proofs to which she had put him.

How unhappy I have rendered him! she exclaimed. *How could he not be in the terrible state to which we see him reduced? How many times I have wounded that delicate and sensitive heart by making him see all of my penchant for a fickle individual so unworthy of being preferred to him, while engaging him to serve him, against himself, and at the expense of his life, which he sacrificed without measure! With what fidelity he employed himself, at the expense of his repose; with what tenderness he felt sorry for me, and afflicted himself for the poor success of his efforts.*

Can such an ardent tenderness be so disinterested, so secret? But after knowing about my involuntary penchant for another who merited it so little, will the gift of my hand and my faith appear capable to him of repaying his tenderness? Can he believe that the gift of my heart will follow it? Forgive me, unfortunate Zoophir, for this dread; it is quite natural; but, too sure of making your happiness, it is impossible that mine is not attached to it.

I loved Thaamar without knowing it and you loved me without me knowing it. But I finally know Thaamar; could I still love him? I know your heart; could I defend myself against loving it? Let your brother go far away from us, to sustain or overturn States; let him depart, and let your candor, your fortunate genius, make my happiness and that of the Empire.

As she had no doubt that Krantor would try to raise obstacles to the course of action she had decided to follow, she sent a person of confidence at that very moment to Nouskirvan to inform him of the resolutions she had formed and the reasons she had for making them and for not changing them. She asked him to recall Prince Thaamar incontinently and without delay, to send an express order of which she could make use to make that prince depart at the moment she judged it appropriate to make use of it. It was on those conditions that she offered him her hand and her crown for Zoophir.

As she finished giving her instructions and her orders, Krantor, followed by the most assiduous members of Thaamar's party among the peers, entered Amasie's apartment.

The old man, once so sage, was beginning to sense the impression of the years. In becoming weaker, he wanted to appear more absolute, and sometimes mingled obstinacy and impatience where he could not supply reasons. The peers that he had contained had commenced to perceive that weakening, and took a high tone alongside him in proportion to the loss of strength of his own, with the result that the deputation of sorts had a tumultuous and conspiratorial air that displeased the princess greatly.

Krantor spoke for a long time without Amasie thinking that she ought to interrupt him. He said and repeated a great deal about the necessity of choosing a husband and a sovereign worthy of Amasie, the advantages of choosing Thaamar, the wishes of the nation for the choice of that prince: everything that he wanted to repeat and say.

When he had ceased, one of those who accompanied him wanted to add to what he had said; the princess listened to him. A second took the floor; he too was heard. A third wanted to speak; she suffered that as well. A fourth was about to commence, but she imposed silence on him, and said to Krantor:

"Sire, I know what I owe to your cares, and I will always conserve a grateful memory of them, but I only owe the scepter I bear to the gods and to my birth; I know that well enough to make anyone remember it who might forget it, however important he might be in my Empire. My subjects are awaiting my choice of a sovereign; my choice will be free and worthy of me; it will be my good fortune and that of the entire nation. It is made; you shall know it in three days. Assemble the leaders of the nation in the usual form; it is in their presence that I shall render my choice public."

Krantor was not accustomed to that proper and absolute tone of the sovereign: a tone that imposes naturally on anyone who is a subject. He gave the example of silence, respect and profound bows with which he and all those who had accompanied him withdrew.

The three days the preceded the one that was to decide the interesting choice that Amasie was to render public passed in all the trouble and agitation imaginable on the part of those who thought they had interests and more or less distant pretentions therein.

Thaamar was not one of the least agitated; he did not expect anything of the favorable dispositions of Amasie since the adventure of Liga, and he also counted little on Krantor and the peers since the response that the princess had made them; his sole resource was in the difficulty he saw in choosing worthily, and in a fashion that could make the good fortune of the nation, in not choosing him.

As for Zoophir, too weak to go out, he was incapable, mentally as well as physically, of taking part in the movements that were agitating so many others. He contented himself with making sincere prayers for the well-being of Amasie and a people who cherished her because she was their sovereign. If he had dared to found any hope on the precise assurances that the princess had seemed to give him, in refusing him Liga's mercy, especially on what she had added since in the various messages sent to seek information of the prince's condition, and if he had not been too modest to flatter himself, the same reasons on which his brother was founding his expectations uniquely would have been sufficient to destroy his hopes. He counted, therefore, on hearing the choice of the popular voice, applauding it publicly and dying of it secretly.

The much-anticipated day finally arrived. The princess had received, the day before, everything that she had requested from Nouskirvan: absolute orders for Thaamar to quit Persia immediately; a consent and good wishes for the happiness and coronation of Zoophir. She immediately wrote a note to that prince conceived in these terms:

Tomorrow I am giving a sovereign to my people; your presence is necessary to me, I know your condition; I am the cause of it. Deliver yourself confidently to all the hope that might change it. It is Amasie who implores you and who orders you to do so. I shall judge your confidence in my prayers and your submission to my orders, by the change that appears in you; and you will see in my eyes a satisfaction proportionate to the miracle that I expect.

Zoophir was so weak on receiving that note, and so troubled by reading it that he could only reply briefly:

Amasie knows that she is adored; can Zoophir do otherwise than obey her?

Hope is, in fact, a very active and very prompt relief for ills of the species of the one from which the prince was about to perish. He was in a deplorable state when he received Amasie's note; he was unable to close an eye all night, and spent it entirely in kissing it and re-reading it, but the next day he seemed so perfectly reestablished that everyone agreed that the change was a prodigy. Many people thought that magic had a part in it. Although Amasie knew how natural the remedy was, she nevertheless admired its potency; the joy that she had promised to let him see in her eyes, in proportion to the miracle, shone there is a fashion that she alone would have been capable of producing.

When all the Orders of the State were assembled in one of the halls of the palace, destined for the indicated ceremony, Amasie came to place herself on her throne. She was superbly dressed and ornamented with all the marks of her dignity, but what shone within her even more than her extreme adornment, more than the diamonds and the precious stones with which she was covered, was her sovereignly majestic air; it was the species of exquisite and singular beauty that suddenly changed her, in the moments when she was ready to carry out an action worthy of the grandeur of her soul or the generosity of her heart.

To her right, on a platform, were Krantor and all the peers and ministers. On the platform to the left were Thaamar, Zoophir and all the foreign princes and lords that were then in Persia.

Krantor, speaking in the name of the nation, invited the queen to fulfill the wishes of her subjects by means of the choice she was about to make, which they desired ardently, by virtue of their sincere attachment to her person; he could not prevent himself saying indirectly two or three words to the advantage of Thaamar, and finished with protestations of submission and respect for the will of a sovereign so dear to her people.

When Krantor had finished speaking a great silence fell. Amasie, her face covered with a noble blush, said: "My first duty is to the love of my people, so my first desire and my unique concern is their happiness; it is more essentially attached to the qualities appropriate to maintain peace that a talent for making war; it is therefore, Zoophir that I choose for my husband and to reign over Persia.

"Come, Prince," she said to Zoophir, getting up and presenting her hand to him with a very good grace, "come and receive the homages and the oath of fidelity of my subjects; and let the foremost," she said, turning toward the platform where Krantor was, "give the first example."

As soon as she had proffered the name of Zoophir, the hall resounded for a long time with acclamations and redoubled cries, which marked the most vivid joy.

Zoophir tried to prostrate himself at the knees of the princess, kissing the hand that she had presented to him; she lifted him up and sat him down to her right.

Then she said to Thaamar: "Prince, I know that my crown, without my hand, would have made your happiness, but my hand without my crown would have made your brother's; unable to separate those gifts, it is just that he unites them; see his happiness, therefore, less as a hero than as a brother. Nouskirvan has requested me to render you to his tenderness, and to his Estates, which have need of your support; receive the orders to do so in his own hand; he has confided them to me in order to convey them to you; but only carry them out as late as is possible for you."

Until that moment, it had been easy to remark, in spite of the general and public satisfaction, that all the members of Thaamar's party had been nonplussed and consternated. Even Krantor, although he had presented himself first and without any delay, at the foot of the throne, in order to make the oath, had not manifested the delight of an aged uncle and former guardian who approves of what his pupil is doing; he had conserved a distracted and pensive expression, which some of the visages of the ministers and the peers had taken as their model.

Scarcely had the princess spoken to Thaamar, however, and shown him Nouskirvan's orders after she had finished speaking, than the prince performed an action that changed all the faces of his party. He leapt down lightly from the platform on which he was placed, and, in a very respectful manner, which was also very cheerful, he prostrated himself at the knees of the princess, who took great care in lifting him up and presenting him to Zoophir. The two brothers embraced very tenderly, several times.

Then the acclamations recommenced; the joy was no longer equivocal, and all the faces cleared. Krantor himself, seeing Thaamar's expression of satisfaction, overbid the public joy, and appeared as content as he had initially appeared discontented. Everyone applauded Thaamar's action sincerely, and found it the best he had done since arriving in Persia.

Zoophir and Amasie were conducted to the Temple of the Sun, where they were united, and their happiness was all the more real because it was felt by all their subjects, who delivered themselves for several days to the insensate joy and intoxication of a sort that there is no need to command of them and impossible to impede when it is sincere.

Thaamar quit Persia without regret, on seeing how his brother was loved there, and how much he loved Amasie. In fact, the passion of the latter prince was such that it seemed ever-increasing, even though it always seemed extreme to the point that no further augmentation was possible—with the result that Amasie would have had every reason to congratulate herself for having been able to prefer a prince she had animated to a prince she had loved. She found that it is impossible for a virtuous princess not to attach herself tenderly to a husband by whom she is cherished perfectly; whereas it is very possible to await in vain the return of a fickle prince.

Krantor lived long enough to be convinced that his niece had known far better than him in what her happiness and that of her people consisted; no government more sage had ever been more fortunate and respected. The names of Zoophir and Amasie were proffered as a symbol of peace, concord, justice, tranquility and abundance.

Fortunate are the subjects of a Philosopher King; they are sheltered from revolutions, to which the passions of a sovereign often expose an entire people; they never experience the yoke and the weight of dependency, but savor its tranquility and mildness. But more fortunate still is the king whom sagacity has taken care to form, whom it guides and enlightens. Justice precedes it and peace follows it; their influence, which surrounds him, spreads out and is communicated to the least of his subjects; whatever he commands, it is confidence that executes and love that obeys. Into whatever place of his domination his eyes strays, he sees no desert regions or uncultivated and desolate fields; the active laborer, certain of his harvest, plunges the plowshare and traces the furrows ardently; his flocks fatten and multiply, because the enemy soldier and the exactor do not come to steal them. No subject of that fortunate Empire would want to cease to be, and neighboring peoples desire to become so; they hasten competitively to transport their family and their abode into a climate so fortunate, beneath a sky so mild.

Thus Persia soon became, when the wisdom of Zoophir was combined with that of Amasie. They made few laws, but they were so clear and so sage that it was sufficient to propose them to make them understood and to determine people to follow them.

Krantor died heaped with honors, satisfaction and years, taking with him the sincere regrets of Zoophir, Amasie and all of Persia.

Meanwhile, Zoophir loved his dear princess with an ardor and a constancy superior to all those about which one can read in books, or of which one has heard tell, or even those than can be imagined. The cares of the Empire, the immense detail of affairs, the necessity of representation, and the taste for study—in a word, everything that might at least distract the passion of an ordinary lover—had no purchase on the passion of that unique and singular husband. He found the time to love incessantly, to say so, and to prove it with the same exactitude as if he had had nothing to do.

The Censor Mirror had become, for him, an Apologist Mirror, only occupied with eulogies to his constancy, his tenderness and his fidelity, proof against anything, while rendering account of the enticements offered to the prince—for they were offered; Amasie's court would not have been a court without that, so they were ardent and continual. The mirror reported them all, but it was never able to say that the prince had responded to any of them; often, it deposed that he had not even perceived them.

Thus, the fortunate Amasie enjoyed the rarest of all benefits: the perfect certainty of being veritably loved, and for herself—a benefit that no mortal had enjoyed before her, nor has any since. There is a point at which everyone whose loves is suspended between dread and hope; either people flatter themselves or are needlessly anxious; what would one not give to emerge from those doubts? For that, the enchanter's mirror would be necessary, and no one has it.

All the princesses who had had it before Amasie had found themselves somewhat ill-served in possessing it, instead of which it had enabled enlightenment and happiness until the moment that became decisive.

The fatal year, the year in which the constancy of the spouses united with the Queens of Persia was to decide their fate or that of the mirror, ran to its end; in a short time it was about to elapse; only a few days remained to pass in order to attain the last hour, but a few days are so long, and can be so dangerous when it is a matter of the constancy of a husband. What does it require to see all the fruit of an expiring year devastated? An instant, the blink of an eye, nothing and less than nothing, and an accursed mirror ready to break becomes as hard as bronze, as diamond.

They went by, however, those critical days, which made me tremble so many times for my dear Amasie. The prince, who must have been a rare model of constancy and conjugal faith, furnished gloriously his career of fidelity, complete and very pure, until the final moment of the final hour, so the mirror did not break partially and as if regretfully; it was not a slight, equivocal crack, which could be attributed to hazard or an accident. It was not a little shard in a corner of the glass; it was the entire mass that was pulverized and shattered, annihilated with all the accompaniment appropriate to decorate a great event, with an enormous din, piercing flashes, swirls of fire of every color, and a thick smoke reeking of bitumen and sulfur.

A few people worthy of faith assured me afterwards that they had heard long whistles, the cries of hobgoblins; that they had seen, through the fire and the smoke with which the apartment was completely filled, frightful faces similar to those that Callot has imagined; but that is a point that merits confirmation, because, once the imagination is stimulated, it sees many things that it invents itself and which only exist therein.

At any rate, perhaps there had never been so many people gathered around that mirror as there were at that moment, and never had they been so far away from it and less occupied with it.

Amasie and Zoophir, who often assembled scholars of every sort; they were then surrounded by them. The conference that took place in another apartment had been moved that day to the cabinet because a few repairs were being made to the assembly room.

All those scholars, occupied with a very delicate point of doctrine, were arguing with one another, not giving a thought to the mirror, although they were looking at it, when it shattered. Their fear was great at first, although they did not want to admit that subsequently; when those messieurs reasoned coldly after the fact about the causes, they made a semblance of not having been frightened by the effects, for the simple reason that they were able to discuss the causes, but in truth, at the moment when the alarming effects struck them, they were scarcely thinking about causes; their knowledge fled and fear clawed them as it would the most ignorant of people.

As soon as the initial terror had passed, the idea that came to all those composing the assembly, was that lightning had just struck, before their eyes, that ancient item of furniture of the Queens of Persia. Perhaps that phenomenon would have given rise to a dissertation, which might have become interesting; but that was prevented by what followed: a soft light, increasing by degrees, like that of the dawn, pierced and soon dissipated entirely the swirls of smoke with which the apartment was full.

An exquisite odor, composed of unknown perfumes, took the place of the reek of sulfur and bitumen by which the sense of smell had been affected. A symphony and melodious voices were heard; the ceiling had disappeared; a pale blue cloud enclosed a chariot hitched to unknown winged animals, and on that chariot was an old man, who appeared to be several thousand years older than anything ordinarily seen on earth. Under his furrowed brow shone eyes full of majesty and softness; his old age had nothing broken or repulsive about it; his beard and his long, floating hair were a dazzling white; a long crimson mantle was attached to his left shoulder by a brilliant diamond of a size one dares not describe, so extraordinary did it appear.

The cloud diminished as he drew nearer, only allowing the chariot and the dragons hitched to it to be seen, which came to alight gently in the apartment, Then the old man, venerable if anyone ever was, emerged from his vehicle much more lightly that the apparent number of his years should have permitted, and bowed profoundly to Zoophir and Amasie, who, without departing from what their rank demanded of them, returned his reverences by means of profound inclinations. When one does not know people and they announce themselves in such a singular fashion, however grand one is, one forgets it; nothing resembles respect better that dread.

The reverences made, the singular phantom traversed the room silently; he went as far as the table on which the mirror had been set. He placed a ring thereon, which had been on one of the fingers of his left hand; then, making a circle around the ring with a small ebony wand that he was holding in his right hand, he pronounced a few unintelligible words in a low voice, and the ring instantly formed a luminous circle in which appeared, as if imprisoned, all the princesses who had possessed the mirror before Amasie: Narbe, Theazir and thirty others. All were ravishingly beautiful, and in the full bloom of youth.

Then a second circle formed alongside the first, containing the princes whose infidelity had conserved the mirror and caused the death or the dolor of the princesses; a lugubrious fire composed that second ring, and the princes had lost their grace and their youth; all of them had expressions of repentance and chagrin.

Then Mirzaf—for no one will have doubted that it was him—placing his wand between the two circles, had no sooner proffered two of the omnipotent words that he knew than the mirror reappeared, as entire as it had been before the event that has just been described. The only striking difference was that the glass was tarnished for Amasie and Zoophir, as well as all those making up their court; it only made them appear any longer like burnished steel that no longer represents objects; whereas the princes and princesses enclosed in the circle, could be seen perfectly therein. It appeared from the cheerful and satisfied expressions of the princesses that they were looking at themselves with pleasure; by contrast, the anxious and chagrined faces of the princess gave reason to think that they were suffering in seeing themselves therein.

The enchanter began, at that moment, to make a very long speech regarding the properties of his mirror; the subject of his vengeance, which had engaged him to make a present of it to Narbe; the dangerous law with which he had accompanied it; and the revolutions that it had occasioned. He related the stories of all the princes and princesses who were in the circles, without sparing them, and without flattering them, indicating them with his wand, in much the same way that our conjurors show the figures that they are about to cause to vanish.

At first, people listened in pure shock, without hearing him; they ended up hearing him with pleasure, because he narrated pleasantly and his manners were mild; besides which, one gets used to everything with time.

His dragons had begun by chilling people with fear because their wings, their claws and their glinting eyes appeared to be a bad augury, but they had crouched down and furled their wings, and when their master had begun to speak they had curled up, rather like the dogs that are harnessed to little carts, and gone to sleep with the best will in the world; apparently, they were accustomed to that conduct, when their master commenced to speak and knew, in their fashion, that it would last for some time.

The enchanter confessed that he had repented of having proposed such a long time for the proof on which the return of his cherished mirror depended; he agreed that he had merited losing it and that he had despaired of ever seeing it again; he ended by giving great eulogies to the constant fidelity of Zoophir; he was sure that it was proof against any magic mirror, and capable of breaking them by the dozen. He predicted for Amasie and her husband a long series of very happy years, and a posterity without number, worthy of them both.

After that, he, his mirror, his circles, his princes and princesses, his chariot and his dragons were all enveloped by a dense cloud and disappeared.

His predictions received a complete accomplishment; Amasie was always loved by Zoophir with an equal tenderness; she gave her husband and her people numerous princes, who were all worthy heirs of the virtues of those to whom they owed the light of day. Those two spouses lived and reigned for many years, uniquely occupied with their reciprocal tenderness and the felicity of their subjects, so their memory is still cherished in their fatherland.

And it is from the name of Zoophir that that of Sophi is formed,[11] which the sovereigns of that Empire have taken since, in the same way that the name of the first Caesar became the title of the Roman Emperors who succeeded him. It is thus that the names of great men become generic names and form a designation and an epithet to which the idea of grandeur remains perpetually attached.

---

[11] I have left the word Sophi as it is given in the original text. The familiar modern equivalent, Sufi, has been hijacked by an Islamic sect, applied to a mystic rather than a wise man in a more general sense. The term was, indeed, a title used for some time by a dynasty of Persian monarchs, but in that context it was a diminutive of Safavid, the name of the dynasty in question, founded in the sixteenth century, rather than representing a claim to wisdom. Contemporary references in English literature—by Shakespeare, for instance—usually rendered it as Sophy. When the present story was written the collapse of the Safavid dynasty, in 1722, was relatively recent.

Appendix:

THE HISTORY AND ADVENTURES OF MILORD PET, AN ALLEGORICAL TALE

To Messieurs the Cesspool-Emptiers of the city and environs of Paris, lords of the base works of the realm, appurtenances and dependencies.

Messieurs, although the noble employment that you exercise does not permit me to approach your redoubtable persons, I dare to present to you, however, from a respectful distance, a work that is within your jurisdiction and which I cannot dedicate to anyone else without injustice. If this book merits your approval, I am assured of that of the public; as everyone is informed of your rare knowledge of the matters that I am treating, every suffrage will the regulated in accordance with yours; for in this matter, at least, what is to your taste is to everyone's taste. Deign, therefore, Messieurs, to have some indulgence toward my work, which can only be treated with dignity by yourselves, if your zeal and occupations for the public good have left you sufficient leisure. If flatter myself that I shall have some part in those depths of bounty that are spread incessantly without being exhausted, and that you will splash back as far as me some portion of the benign influences that everyone senses. It is already a glory for me to have the opportunity to mark publicly the profound veneration with which I have the honor to be, Messieurs, your very humble and very obedient servant,

Jeanne Fesse.

The History of Milord Pet[12]

I offer here the life of a celebrated hero, who has filled the entire earth with the rumor of his name, although it has not always been rendered the justice that it merits; of an extraordinary mortal who, from the bosom of poverty and humiliation has risen to the summit of glory without any other aid than that of merit; of an abortion and simultaneously a prodigy of Nature, which the earth did not judge worthy of her at first and who, gradually rising above the earth, judged in his turn that she was not worthy of him. This history, although short, might become interesting by virtue of the sentiments that the hero might inspire. The obscurity of his name will doubtless not put readers off; a just mind will find him all the greater in his glory because it will have seen that he had further to travel in order to arrive.

I. The Birth of Milord Pet

Milord Pet was born in Culotte, a city in the netherlands, amid the embraces of two two sisters, his cousins, named Fesses. His mother Grosventre did not carry him for long. Great men are formed right away.

He was for his parents a premature fruit, like the forerunner of a quite different son whom they were waiting. That is why they had nothing but scorn at first for

---

[12] It is impossible to understand this story and to decode its many *double entendres* without knowing that *pet* is the French term for a fart.

the unfortunate runt, and even reproached themselves for having brought him into existence. Having been frustrated in their expectation with regard to the second, however, they rendered to him, with the right of the elder, their esteem and their affection.

What gave him above all the preference over his younger brother is that the defects he had brought into the world were always diminishing, whereas they not only persevered with the latter but became ever more insupportable. He also had the advantage that he jabbered from birth, whereas the other remained mute all his life. He was, therefore, brought up in the house under the eyes of his parents, while his brother was repudiated and expelled, never to reappear.

II. The Character of Milord Pet

There was no childhood for our little Milord. Less materialistic than his brother, he became a man almost immediately. He was mild and affable to everyone, but especially toward his parents whom he kissed and caressed incessantly, to the extent of importunity.

It is necessary to say in his praise that he was never ingrate. Liberal toward everyone, his first favors were for those to whom he owed existence. He was extremely talkative and loquacious. Although he knew nothing, there was almost no discussion that he did not interrupt in order to put in a word in his fashion. He was subtle, shrewd and insinuating—for those are virtues among the men of today—but his shrewdness and subtlety were so admirable that he escaped when one thought one had him, and one often had him before one's eyes without perceiving him.

I ought not to dissimulate that he had a few faults. He felt the effects of the baseness of his origin. His mores were not polite; he was prompt and violent, and very few people could boast of not having suffered in the nose and ears when he got carried away. He was also reproached with having bad breath, but that fault was more of nature than education; it would have been overlooked if people were capable of listening to reason when it is a matter of their advantages. He was not reputed to have intelligence, but he must have had prudence, for he always comported himself with weight and measure, and he never did anything without foundation. He was liberal and prodigal to the extent of forcing everyone to accept his services. He was teasing and humorous, and his sallies, piquant for some, amused others. Curious to the point of indiscretion, he wanted to be everywhere, and, which is bad, to spoil and poison everything.

He also had several talents, among others that of persuasion. Scarcely had he spoken than one knew everything that he had to say, with the consequence that a single one of his words was worth an entire speech. He was, however, accused of being secretive, because one could not always grasp him—but that was artfulness rather than deceit, for one could not dispute his frankness. He had a voice, and that talent did him a great deal of honor, as you shall see in due course.

He also had a disposition for playing instruments, and the South Wind, his father having brought him a drum on his return from a certain fair, although he was very young, he was so well able to make use of it that it was understood right away that it would one day be his great talent.

He was able to make those who did not want to like him fear him. He was accused of being vindictive, but that was in the case of a just defense. He only did harm when others wanted to harm him. It is certain that several had reason to resent having made attempts on his liberty; here is an example that confirms that verity, as it proves his valor. I advance it with a good guarantee, like all the other facts of his life.

III. Milord Pet, scorned for his faults, is victorious in a duel sustained at Court

Great talents do not always render themselves estimable, especially when they are effaced by some great fault. There was no childhood for Milord Pet, but he had a youth. He was reckless and irresponsible, liking noise and disorder, with the consequence that the city of Culotte and the entire netherlands sensed the racket that he made. He even let a few signs be glimpsed of derangement and corruption; the bad odor of vice that he spread everywhere announced sufficiently what he had spoiled. He thus became odious and insupportable.

No one wanted to see or hear him anywhere. Even his parents no longer loved him, with the consequence that in a free country he suffered a kind of slavery, and away from his homeland he did not experience Gallican liberty. But Providence, whose cares extend everywhere, contrived him an adventure at the Court which rendered him his liberty, or at least made his servitude milder.

A poor provincial gentleman, who was soliciting a royal pension, having obtained a letter of recommendation for one of the Ministers, wanted to submit it personally. As he was waiting for the success that the document the lord in question was reading ought to have, he perceived that Milord Pet, naturally curious, was trying to slip into the cabinet with him.

That timid and respectful man imagined that it would be a capital crime to introduce a third party into such a serious tête-à-tête, and also feared being unfortunate. He made such great efforts to drive away the importunate and to conceal the combat that he was grievously inconvenienced; for his adversary, repelling and returning all his thrusts upon himself, maltreated him in that duel of sorts and he nearly expired on the battlefield.

He was wounded, especially in the lower abdomen, and by bouts of colic that he had for some time; it was feared that his bowels might be compromised. The Minister, who witnessed that encounter, reported it to the King, who granted the vanquished individual the pension he requested, and the victor his grace, accompanied by a few other favors; for, having examined on the one hand the wrong that had been done to him, and on the other, the inconveniences that might result from an unnatural usage, declared Milord Pet's vengeance just and permissible. In order that no one should be exposed henceforth to the vivacity of his resentments, he ordered that no insult should be made to him henceforth, and that he should be given passports and safe conducts throughout the lands of his obedience.

IV. Milord Pet, Soldier

The order of the King, full of wisdom ad equity, was executed throughout the realm. Milord Pet no longer received as many insults on the part of the French. And, seeing that he was free to travel, he resolved to quit the lowlands, either because he no longer believed himself to be really free, or because he wanted to breathe a purer air. It was time to embrace a status in life; he thought about it maturely, and the profession of arms appearing to him to be most in conformity with his inclination, he joined a Regiment[13] that was garrisoned at Culotte. If it is true that he was as deranged as he was thought to be, he needed that school in order to lose all his faults.

He was received there with pleasure and called Bonne Odeur for his *nom de guerre*. The refreshment that he paid all the soldiers on the day of his entry commenced to make him known, but he distinguished himself above all in the trials of strength that he made some times later by his prodigies of valor, of which no example had been seen before him. He fought alone against all, laying some low and putting the rest to flight; all were frightened and declared themselves defeated. Surprised by so much courage, they could not weary of talking about him, and already feared that he might pass over the belly of all; but he soon degenerated from his initial valor; he had the fault of showing himself everywhere at once instead of making his glory last by being more sparing with it.

The hero almost vanished in showing himself, and all his glory going up in smoke, they saw the one who had announced himself as a hero fleeing like a coward. His fall was all the greater because he had appeared more elevated, and as cowardice cannot be tolerated in a soldier he was expelled from the Corps. He was demot-

---

[13] Author's note: "Which is to say, of Lice." Although the author uses the French term, *poux*, it is possible that he had the English term in mind, because *lice*, in French can mean a battlefield or the area of a tourney.

ed, passed under the flag,[14] and led out of the camp with loud jeers.

V. Milord Pet is made Drum Major

Seeing himself expelled ignominiously from the Corps of Graycoats, Milord Pet or Bonne Odeur quit the city of Culotte for good and all, where many ill-treatments had caused him to experience the verity of the proverb that no one is generally esteemed in his own country.

He traversed the long Spine Plains, here he encountered a regiment of Amazons,[15] composed of several battalions. They were at war with the great Master of the World,[16] and had already taken possession of several fortified places. He examined the order of their march and the conduct of their operations for some time. Some of them were garrisoned in the fortresses, others were scouting. He was charmed by their lightness.

He marched while beating the big drum, for we have already remarked that he had had a taste for that instrument since childhood. The Amazons, naturally flighty, had need of a drummer to assemble them when necessary; they proposed that employment to him, which he accepted. It was easy for him to distinguish himself therein, having been born with that talent and always having cultivated it. He could be heard all over the camp, and even all over the plain.

He brought back anyone on the Corps neglectful of their duty by means of his chamades. He recalled the

---

[14] Author's note: "Which is to say, the chemise."

[15] Author's note: "Which is to say, of Fleas."

[16] Author's note: "Which is to say, Man."

marauders, for they made abundant use of that tactic at the expense of their enemy. He animated everyone in combat, and alerted them when it was necessary to mount an assault. It is even said that, taking his cares beyond his employment, he served them as a supplier and distributed certain refreshments from time to time that were much to their taste. In a word, he was liked, and he would have been happy in that employment if he had been able to stick to it—or, rather, if his ambition had permitted him to be content with it. He therefore formed the resolution to desert, and carried it out, but he had a good deal of difficulty, for he found all the avenues of that long plain closed, and he needed all his suppleness to cross the barriers that had doubtless been raised in order to stop him.

VI. Milord Pet is vanquished by a Devotee

By what I have just said, it can easily be judged that Milord Pet did not like women. He even had some reason not to like them, for that sex had always affected an aversion for him, although it is said that the hatred was only external, and that in secret it was less disgusted, because it is a routine modesty among women to disguise their amours under an apparent indifference. At any rate, there was always at least an exterior antipathy between women and Milord Pet. They even appeared to be perpetually at war. He obtained several advantages over them, and victory escaped them sometimes when they thought they had it, which rendered them more confused. But he was vanquished in his turn one day, and it was a Devotee who had that glory. The event appears to me to be too amusing to pass over in silence.

Petronille, a Sister of the Third Order, was ensconced one day in a respectable place, applied to the reading of a book recently composed by Père Janvier,[17] a Capuchin, a forceful director whose nickname was the Pocket Pistol for the Assassination of Mortal Sin. That was all the reason necessary to fix her attention and render the reading agreeable. Milord Pet attempted to distract her from it, doubtless to mortify her self-esteem. The Master of the place would have stopped that temeritous individual if he had had reason enough to make the difference.

Although he came from behind, he could not hide his steps and his preparation from Petronille; nothing escapes the eyes of Devotees. She disposed herself to combat that enemy worthy of her, and dispute the passage, under the pretext that he was a profanity that ought to be banished from the temple and altars. She was known far and wide for her zeal, which had already borne her to other exploits of that nature.

However, the enemy had momentum, and was already on the heels of the alarmed Devotee, who, by virtue of the contortions the combat caused her to make and the twitches that she endured, appeared to the witnesses either to be assailed by some violent temptation or to be disposing herself for some display of fanaticism. In the end she remained partially victorious; at least, she avoided the noise and the scandal. Her enemy was obliged to escape as a timid fugitive, and to mark her victory, she condemned him to silence.

---

[17] Père Janvier [Father January] remains an alternative term in France for Père Noël [Father Christmas], of whom he was a folkloristic predecessor in some provinces.

Confused by such a shameful defeat, he avenged himself without explosion, but fully. He infected the air with the black vapors that he trails after him, and as he had remained on the battlefield, he left everywhere, in passing, the odor of an already rotted cadaver. Our pious heroine did not remain there, far from being swelled with pride by that victory, scruples took possession of her mind and she believed herself to be culpable of a kind of murder. She had heard mention in veiled terms of a horrible crime committed by a young woman, which she was simple enough to confound with her own.

She commenced with a rude flagellation to avenge herself on her backside. That is always the weak party. The unfortunate is always the culpable and the victim, especially so on this occasion. Afterwards, unable to remain charged with such a burden for long, she ran to vomit the monster at the feet of her confessor. But as it was a singular caution, she did not know how to express herself in order to make her crime known.

Finally, uttering a deep sigh, she said to him: "Father, I accuse myself of having strangled my fruit."

One can imagine the surprise of Père Janvier, who understood the force of terms better. He was disconcerted at first, but having put two and two together and seeing the poor young woman's error, he said: "Go in peace; provided that you did not extinguish the lamps in the church, God will pardon you and I will absolve you."

VII. Milord Pet, Musician

One cannot deny that Milord Pet had great qualities to make a hero; he was brave and bold,[18] facing danger

---

[18] Author's note: "Intrepid."

instead of fearing it; his blows never miscarried; he always hit the target on the nose and never missed his man. But he fought without regulation and without prudence; a fault that rendered all his talents futile. Content to vanquish, he did not care where his darts landed; he punished his friends as well as his enemies, with the result that his valor was always deadly to those of his own party; that is what provides consolation for the loss of such a soldier when he quits a corps.

He finally lost his taste for the profession of arms, perhaps chagrined by no longer seeing himself applauded therein. He returned to France, where he knew that people would be pleased to see him, and having quit the sword he finally dedicated himself to music. He did not pass through the ordinary channels, but without any other principles than those he had received from nature, he suddenly became a musician—or, rather, pretended to be. He had a voice, as we have said; he even knew how to control it; and what seems strange is that he sang with some taste, making everything that he pronounced felt so forcefully that hearing was not the only sense affected by his sounds.[19]

---

[19] The author of this story could have had no idea, of course, that Joseph Pujol (1857-1945) , nicknamed Le Pétomane, would one day achieve great fame in France as a flatulist, inhaling air and then exhaling it at will by means of his anal sphincter; initially demonstrating his talent to fellow soldiers during his obligatory military service, he eventually became highly successful stage performer, making his debut in Marseille in 1887 and appearing at the Moulin Rouge in Paris in 1892; after falling out with the management of that establishment he started his own traveling show, the Théâtre Pompadour, composing his own eccentric music as well as playing the Marseillaise and other well-known tunes. He could also

He took with him a troupe of workless vagabonds, and, animating that idle and impotent band unaided, he formed a Musical corps that as known as the vagabond orchestra. There, everyone played his part—or, rather, it was Milord Pet who played them all; he alone provided the vocal and instrumental music; and what is remarkable is that although the spectators could not see any instrument, they seemed to hear them all, for Milord, who imitated the serpent and the bassoon perfectly, was also able to accommodate the soft tones of the flute and the flageolet.

Their songs were all in honor of Crepitus[20] and Bacchus, so they were well matched to those sorts of deities. Taverns were the ordinary temples where their motets were performed; their confused and masculine songs resounded there day and night; in particular, the orchestra snored marvelously and prevailed over voices. Jealous of their glory, they neglected nothing to succeed in their concerts. Not only did they take care to drink heavily, like all other singers, but they also used certain legumes, such as beans, and other that could give them a voice, according to experiments they had carried out.

Furthermore, they were so attached to the gods they served that they did not neglect anything that could con-

---

blow out a candle at a distance of several meters. Allegedly horrified by the atrocities of the Great War, he retired from the stage and reverted to his former profession as a baker, founding a biscuit factory in Toulon. One might be tempted to say that you couldn't make it up—except, as the present story demonstrates, someone already had.

[20] Author's note: "The god of latrines." The medical meaning of the term *crepitus* had been invented in 1755, but it was effectively confined to Latin treatises, thus leaving the word free for this fanciful reattribution.

tribute to their glory; and, combining worship with praise, they accompanied their songs with frequent incense, in which the audience could have participated but in which, either out or respect or delicacy they refused to share. The incense therefore rose with the sounds, they were lost in the air together, and attracted to them by way of recompense an admirable fecundity.

Milord Pet was retained in that corps, of which he was the soul and the leader, for a long time. The glory that he acquired there and the applause that he received flattered his self-esteem; people ran to that music as to a novelty, and his talents, by which people had previously been horrified, were admired, as long as they were rare, so true is it that one is esteemed in any genre, provided that one excels therein.

However, our musician was lost in those excesses; his voice enfeebled by debauchery, he sang even more, but he did not sing as strongly; he needed to diet for a few days to inflate his tones. He therefore quit his band, which he already regarded as unworthy of him, but with the promise to see them again from time to time, and to lend then his services occasionally.

VIII. Milord Pet, Physician

Although music was to Milord Pet's taste, it did not content his ambition. He resolved to make it his amusement, but not his occupation. Born for glory and elevation, he needed a more honorable estate, and he was searching for one when a very singular adventure suddenly made him a physician, without any of the ordinary formalities, a profession in which he nevertheless distinguished himself, although he never received a doctoral qualification.

A young and robust peasant having presented himself in an assembly for some affair, first made his salutation as best he could, but then, either out of timidity or ignorance, he was unable to say a single word to express his commission. Milord Pet, seeing his embarrassment, spoke for him, but in a tone so firm that everyone was astounded by it.

Attempts were made to oblige the man to retire, or at least to dismiss his interpreter, but then, recovering the power of speech and suddenly becoming eloquent, he said: "I'm very sorry; the necessity is too great for me; as long as I have him with me, I have no fear of maladies. People do not know the merit of that physician; he's a pearl in a dung-heap. See my plumpness; it's the effects of his cares and his visits. Every word that he speaks is a sign of life, and his presence alone is a specific."

Having said that, he went out as he had come in: the same escape; the same compliment. They were indignant at his recidivism, but after having reflected on what he had said, the confirmation of which was borne in his face, they no longer criticized him as much.

"In truth," said a demoiselle of the company, "I believe that man is right; with all our ceremonies and refinements, we are only seeking what is contrary to our wellbeing. I did not reject that physician in my childhood, and I was in good health, whereas, now that I have been given the lesson to avoid him, I have jaundice, as if he wanted to avenge himself for my scorn."

"I think as you do," added an old man whose opinion was respected. "I did not know maladies in the days when I was young and less serious, and made it a pleasure to converse with him, where as they all seem to afflict me since I have made a delicacy out of hearing him.

We hinder ourselves in hindering him, and what are we avoiding, after all, but a little urgency that he is accustomed to make in his visits? The noise is not the most disagreeable thing about him. Why not accept people with their faults, especially when they are useful to us?"

Everyone applauded; it was agreed to make a trial of the remedy, and having done so, it was found to be so good, and so many eulogies were given to Milord Pet, that he immediately became celebrated and fashionable; for everything in the world has its vicissitudes, especially in France, in order, as a faithful historian, not to betray verity. There was no more talk of anything but him and his cures. Desired everywhere for his secrets, present everywhere by virtue of his lightness, he relieved some, cured others and even resuscitated a few.

A curé worthy of belief has assured me that, while burying one of his parishioners one day, he was astonished to hear all the people crying out at once: "Stop, don't bury that man yet; the great physician is arriving; he'll resuscitate him." And, indeed, Milord Pet only had to appear, whisper a few words in the ear, presented a few scents to the nose, and the dead man immediately began to respire and speak, as if he wanted to respond to his benefactor. Everyone cried miracle, all the more so because he effected that cure, like all the others, without expense and without preparation; his presence alone, as if by an admirable sympathy, rendered health or life.

He nevertheless prescribed a certain regime of life; he counseled frugality, and a strict diet; he permitted wine, but without excess; and when people were exact in following his advice, he rendered to invalids and alerted them with that air of assurance that announces a cure, whereas he came gently and as if partially when his prescription was not carried out.

He had too much glory not to excite envy. All of Pharmacy was unleashed against him and made open war on him. Physicians and engineers strove to evacuate the fortresses he occupied and had mines hollowed out wherever he passed.[21] Surgeons employed an arsenal of small arms against him that were no less dangerous, and apothecaries were deputized to mount an assault. They did not lack courage. What can a man not do when he is fighting for his interests? They laid low the entire city of Culotte, and turned a part of Holland[22] upside down. They presented themselves before the breach with various species of small caliber cannons[23] in order to force the enemy into his retrenchments, and in spite of the defense put up by that generous besieged individual from the depths of the fortress, they made their discharge with incredible firmness.

In order to aim their cannons better they knelt down, and the majority put on large spectacles that also served them as armor against enemy arrows. In the end, as a last resource, they opened the floodgates, following the example of the Dutch, and inundated he camp of the besieged, who were obliged to make a few sorties, always to the disadvantage of the besiegers, having left, however, a good garrison in the fortress—with the result

---

[21] Author's note: "By nurses and other remedies they prescribed."

[22] Author's note: "Which is to say, the chemise." (In the sense of Holland linen, although the connection to the Netherlands is evident.)

[23] Author's note: "Which is to say, syringes." The reference is not to hypodermic syringes but to devices for administering enemas.

that, weary of obstinate and fruitless toil, the latter lifted the siege and withdrew, vanquished and confused.

IX. Milord Pet at the French Court

I ought not to pass over in silence the fuss that was made of Milord Pet at Court, not only when his name became celebrated, but even when it was still obscure. There were princes and lords who begged him for his protection even in his disgrace. It does not count for little in the glory of our hero that the illustrious capital in question has recognized his merit. The judgment of that Mistress of the Arts could compensate him for the scorn of other cities; perhaps he had appealed to that respectable tribunal, as a last resort, against their injustice.

There is no one who has not heard mention of the Duc de R**.[24] He made so much fuss of him that he took him into his service, so to speak, and often admitted him to his table. What proves that he had some with is that he was able to amuse and cause to laugh the man who amused and made the whole court laugh, with the result that he was a kind of jester to the king's jester. I could confirm what I advance by means of several known facts; here is one that might amuse the reader.

The Duc de R** had invited an ambassador to a ceremonial meal, at which Milord Pet as not present.

---

[24] Armand de Vignerot du Plessis, Duc de Richelieu (1696-1788)—the conclusion to which contemporary readers would immediately have leapt. The Duc was Louis XV's best friend for many years, although the relationship cooled in the 1750s because of the king's relationship with Madame de Pompadour, of whom Richelieu disapproved.

That lord took it into his head to drag along Père Rot,[25] a hideous and dirty monsieur as much detested in France as he is liked in certain countries. At the first sight of him the Duc was offended, and testified his discontent to the ambassador by means of the grave and serious expression he adopted, contrary to his custom. Meanwhile, he alerted Milord Pet to be ready to appear if the foreign monster was not sent away.

The E**[26] were too proud to yield. The indiscreet guest persisted in retaining Père Rot at table, and even affected to place him under the Duc's nose. The latter, seeing insolence pushed to the end, had Milord Pet advance, who saluted his gravity in a firm and bold tone and reproached him for his impoliteness. Then, having made contact with Père Rot, they found themselves to be related, although emerging from another branch, and born in a different realm.

The ambassador, unable to suffer such a guest facing him, got up, expressing his discontentment, and immediately went to carry his complaint to the king and demand a reckoning.

He was heeded. The Duc was obliged to make a reparation, but a sally got him out of their affair. "Let us have the parties kiss and make up," he said, "let bygones be bygones and be better friends than ever."

Everyone applauded that ingenious defeat. Even the ambassador could not help laughing, and declared himself satisfied in favor of the quip.

---

[25] In French, *faire un rot* is vulgar terminology for belching.

[26] Presumably Espagnols [Spaniards].

X. Milord Pet aspires to Royalty

Milord Pet's sojourn in the Court only stimulated his ambition further. Everything that he saw in that great Theater of Human Nobility piqued his spirit of competition. On seeing a hero, he wanted to be a hero; on seeing a king, he wanted to reign.

Already celebrated by virtue of a few victories he had won, battle-hardened by his first exploits, medicine had no more attractions for him. He inclined toward the glory of arms. He preferred the sword to the robe, for heroism has something flattering for great souls.

Remembering then that he had pretentions to the Realm of the Nose, he set forth to conquer it. That country, situated on a height, in rather difficult of access, but ambition gave him wings, and nature having made him more apt to rise than to descend he arrived there in very little time. Those estates, which the right of birth had given to him, had been occupied—or, rather, usurped— by a tyrant named Tobacco, who, no longer knowing the legitimate master and believing himself to be in tranquil possession, took little care to guard his fortresses. Milord Pet therefore found them open, as if abandoned.

The conquest was neither difficult nor glorious; but as there were two avenues of entry he divided his squadron into two corps, like a skillful general, in order that the fortresses would be provided in case of attack.

General Tobacco, alerted to the irruption that had been made into his estates, marched diligently upon the enemy. Both of the pretenders seemed to be well-founded in demanding that realm, one alleging natural right and the other usage and prescription. It was therefore necessary that force was disposed, and that was what concluded the dispute. The two armies often came to grips, and were alternately victorious.

Their forces were equal; they were both composed of men so small that there was reason to give them the name of atoms, but they were so prompt and so subtle that they seemed to participate in the lightness of spirits. The country was, therefore, a theater of war for a long time. One battle was the prelude to another, a victory announced a defeat, with the consequence that each king only enjoyed his estates momentarily in order to have the chagrin of losing them and the shame of being expelled.

While the two armies where thus reduced to consuming one another gradually by checks and being rallied by further reinforcements, General Tobacco made an alliance with Princess Perfume, in which, by ceding to a part of the estates in litigation to her, he obliged her to enter into his defense. Outnumbered by that means, Milord Pet withdrew by virtue of prudence, but without renouncing entirely the right that he had to that terrain, to which he returned from time to time, to alarm his rival with light skirmishes.

XI. The End of Milord Pet

Expelled from his estates without the hope of being able to reenter them, Milord Pet led a sad and languid life on earth. That abode eventually displeased him, and he resolved to quit it. It is said that he found nothing there that was worthy of him, that he regarded it as a place of exile and misery for him, being made for a different fortune. What is certain is that he gradually drew away, and, finally elevating himself by his virtue, with the help of his father, the South Wind, he was lost in the atmosphere; and as he entered that new region, his heart seemed to dilate, as if it were arriving at its center.

This would be the finest part of the history if the human mind could penetrate the secrets of the heavens; it is said, however, that Milord Pet, after having quit the earth, presented himself before the Council of the Gods, and, having made the most of his titles of Child of the Wind and of the Earth, he succeeded in proving sufficiently in proving his divine origin. The gods having reproached him for having degenerated, however, he could not justify himself. Crepitus, in order to recompense his services, wanted to make him a subaltern divinity or demigod, but all the other gods, with a common voice, opened for establishing him as the minister of their vengeance, confiding him to the care of the Thunder—which he accepted gladly, in order to have the opportunity in that employment to avenge himself on the earth for the scorn he claimed to have received there.

CLASSIC FRENCH FANTASY

Honoré de Balzac. *The Last Fay*
Gabrielle-Suzanne Barbot de Villeneuve. *The Naiads Beauty and The Beast*
Chevalier de Béthune. *The World of Mercury*
Jean Carrère. *The End of Atlantis*
Charlotte-Rose Caumont de La Force. *The Land of Delights*
Comte de Caylus. *The Impossible Enchantment*
Félicien Champsaur. *Pharaoh's Wife*
Jacques Collin de Plancy. *Voyage to the Center of the Earth*
Gaston Danville. *The Perfume of Lust*
Comtesse D.L. *The Tyranny of the Fays Abolished*
Paul Féval. *Anne of the Isles*
Charles de Fieux. *Lamékis*
Judith Gautier. *Isoline and the Serpent-Flower*
Nathalie Henneberg. *The Green Gods*
Gustave Kahn. *The Tale of Gold and Silence*
Edmond Haraucourrt. *Dieudonat*
Françoise Le Marchand. *Florine and Boca*
Marie-Jeanne L'Héritier de Villandon. *The Robe of Sincerity*
André Lichtenberger. *The Centaurs; The Children of the Crab*
J-M. & Randy Lofficier. *The French Fantasy Treasury 1-3*
Charles Lomon & P.-B. Gheuzi. *The Last Days of Atlantis*
Maurice Magre. *The Marvelous Story of Claire d'Amour; The Call of the Beast; Priscilla of Alexandria; The Angel of Lust; The Mystery of the Tiger; The Poison of Goa; Lucifer; The Blood of Toulouse; The Albigensian Treasure; Jean de Fodoas; Melusine; The Brothers of the Virgin Gold*
Marie-Madeleine de Lubert. *Princess Camion.*
Camille Mauclair. *The Virgin Orient*
Hippolyte Mettais. *Paris Before the Deluge*
Victor-Emile Michelet. *Superhuman Tales*
Henriette-Julie de Murat. *The Palace of Vengeance*

Charles Nodier. *Trilby   The Crumb Fairy*
Edgar Quinet. *The Enchanter Merlin*
Henri de Régnier. *A Surfeit of Mirrors*
Restif de la Bretonne. *The Fay Ouroucoucou* (2 vols.)
J.-H. Rosny Aîné. *Pan's Flute*
Marie-Anne de Roumier-Robert. *The Voyage of Lord Seaton to the Seven Planets*
Nicolas Ségur. *Penelope's Secret*
Brian Stableford (ed.). *Funestine; The Queen of the Fays*
Kurt Steiner. *Ortog*
C.-F. Tiphaigne de La Roche. *Amilec   Giphantia*
Simon Tyssot de Patot. *The Strange Voyages of Jacques Massé and Pierre de Mésange*